THe

STORY OF A WIDOW

a novel by

MUSHARRAF ALI FAROOQI

alfred A. knopf canada

PUBLISHED BY ALFRED A. KNOPF CANADA

Copyright © 2008 Musharraf Ali Farooqi

All rights reserved under International and Pan-American Copyright
Conventions. No part of this book may be reproduced in any form
or by any electronic or mechanical means, including information
storage and retrieval systems, without permission in writing from the
publisher, except by a reviewer, who may quote brief passages in a
review. Published in 2008 by Alfred A. Knopf Canada, a division
of Random House of Canada Limited. Distributed by
Random House of Canada Limited, Toronto.

Knopf Canada and colophon are trademarks.

www.randomhouse.ca

LIBRARY AND ARCHIVES CANADA CATALOGUING IN PUBLICATION

Farooqi, Musharraf, 1968–
The story of a widow / Musharraf Ali Farooqi.

ISBN 978-0-307-39718-8

I. Title.

PS8611.A76S86 200   C813'.6   C2008-901235-6

Text design: Terri Nimmo

First Edition

Printed and bound in the United States of America

2 4 6 8 9 7 5 3 1

For my mother
Tanveer Fatima Farooqi

CONTENTS

CHARACTERS

MONA	*The widow*
AKBAR AHMAD	*Mona's deceased husband*
AMBER	*Mona's younger daughter*
ANEESA	*Mona's aunt*
MRS. BAIG	*Mona's friend and neighbour*
BANO	*Mona's maid-servant*
FARAZ	*Mona's son-in-law, Tanya's husband*
HABIB	*Mona's cook*
HINA	*Mona's elder sister*
HUDA	*A barrister, Mona's lawyer*
IMAD	*An architect, Jafar's cousin*
JAFAR	*Mona's brother-in-law, Hina's husband*
KAMAL	*Mona's son-in-law, Amber's husband*
MRS. KAZI	*Mother-in-law of Mona's daughter, Tanya*
MAHA	*Mona's grand-daughter, Amber and Kamal's daughter*
NOORI	*Mona's maidservant*
RUBAB	*Mona's cousin, Sajid Mir and Aneesa's unmarried daughter*
SAJID MIR	*Mona's uncle*
SALAMAT ALI	*Mona's second husband*
TANYA	*Mona's elder daughter*
UMAR SHAFI	*Mona's second cousin*
ZAIN	*Mona's grand-son, Tanya and Faraz's son*

P r o l o g u e

AKBAR AHMAD WAS FELLED by a stroke one year before his retirement from the finance ministry and three days after being diagnosed with high cholesterol. He was fifty-nine years old. His wife and daughters blamed his untimely demise on excessive eating, his only acknowledged vice. The family remembered him in all other respects as a model of righteousness.

Akbar Ahmad acquitted himself in his posthumous affairs in the same methodical manner in which he had conducted his life. Ordained by the will, his death triggered visits by the lawyer, the accountant and the manager of the local bank. All matters of his estate were discharged before the forty days of ritual mourning were over, and for the first time, his widow, Mona, found herself in charge of finances.

While sorting a drawer of Akbar Ahmad's effects, Mona discovered a photograph taken when he received a citation on the occasion of his twenty-fifth year in service. The portrait accurately captured Akbar Ahmad's sombre persona. Mona had the picture enlarged and framed, then hung it in the living room where she often spent time. When she looked at the portrait, she felt Akbar Ahmad was still with her.

One day when she looked at the portrait, she considered how blessed she had been in life. She contemplated her good fortune in finding an upright man like Akbar Ahmad as her life partner and felt grateful for his bounteous legacy, which released her from all financial cares. Akbar Ahmad looked back at her, his face cast in an expression of long suffering. Mona's eyes welled up with tears.

```
┌─────────┐
│  ┌───┐  │
│  │ I │  │
│  └───┘  │
└─────────┘
```

THE WIDOW

After Akbar Ahmad's death, Mona became more conscious of her own health. She was fifty, and the doctor had warned her about the physical changes she must expect at her age. Her older daughter Tanya insisted that Mona start exercising, so Mona began going for walks in a nearby park every few days with her neighbour from across the street, Mrs. Baig. Often her back felt stiff when she woke up in the mornings, and her legs cramped if she sat in one place for too long. When she looked at Akbar Ahmad's portrait, she was reminded of one of his favourite sayings: It's all the toll and suffering of life!

Mona's chief memories of thirty-one years of married life concerned caring for her husband, raising her two daughters and running a busy household. Akbar Ahmad's steady rise through the ranks of the finance ministry forced him to spend more and more time at work; his weekends were taken up by visits either to his superiors or from his colleagues in the ministry. Over the course of his career, Akbar Ahmad's work engagements overtook his married life. During Akbar Ahmad's last years, a month before the federal budget was announced, his whole office staff numbering six people moved into their house. Akbar Ahmad found it more convenient to work the extra hours from the comfort of his home. Mona and the cook, Habib, remained busy in the kitchen all day, making tea for the staff every few hours and cooking and serving food to them during lunch and dinner. Mona got respite only late at night when the staff left. Still, she had to wash and put away the dishes as Habib would leave soon after the dinner was served.

With Akbar Ahmad occupied by his work, Mona lavished all her attention and care on her first child, Tanya. Three years later their second daughter, Amber, was born, and Mona underwent a prolonged depression. Her older sister, Hina, who attended to her in those days, worried about Mona. She had had a similar episode once before, too, after their father's death. Hina was greatly relieved to notice that despite her low spirits, Mona seemed able to discharge her duties as a mother. However, Mona lost all desire to go outdoors and no longer asked Akbar Ahmad to take time out from work for an outing or a picnic as she had done after the birth of Tanya.

Soon afterwards Akbar Ahmad was posted for a year to Islamabad, a thousand kilometres away from Karachi. He decided that it would be best for Mona to stay behind in Karachi to look after the house and the children. Mona took stock of her circumstances and realized that she had to make an effort to cast off her depression and strike a balance between her needs and the needs of her family. When Akbar Ahmad returned, he apparently never felt anything had been amiss in the household routines. He found his shaving water ready in the morning as before, his office clothes on the bedside in the correct order with the socks on top, and the folded newspaper on the right side of the breakfast table.

Akbar Ahmad liked to have more than one freshly made dish at each meal, with a homemade dessert afterwards. His characteristic frugality lapsed only in the matter of food, so in time he told Mona that they could hire a cook. That was how Habib was hired—their first household help. Afterwards, it turned out that Habib had lied about his long experience. The only dishes he could make with any competence were rice and lentils. It took Mona several months before Habib was properly trained. But his job mostly remained limited to that of kitchen help. Mona was unable to entirely delegate the cooking part. The glimmer of delight in Akbar Ahmad's eyes as she announced the menu she had prepared gave her a sense of fulfillment.

Mona's daytime routine was hardly over when it was time for Akbar Ahmad to come home. Another set of routines would then start: bringing him a hot towel to wipe his face, making tea and pouring it for him after exactly three minutes of steeping, laying the dinner table, and placing three toothpicks and a small hand towel near his plate. When she left a task to Habib, something invariably went wrong, and Akbar Ahmad complained about it for days afterwards.

Mona followed the same household schedule with little variance until the day Akbar Ahmad died.

One of the first changes Mona felt was the sudden end to the daily duties she performed for Akbar Ahmad. After many months of feeling unsettled, she began enjoying her leisure. If she read a book, often she would become so engrossed in it that she forgot about her lunch. When Habib was away, she felt too lazy to prepare meals for herself. On those occasions, only if her daughters or sister dropped by did she make lunch or dinner. Some days she drank pot after pot of jasmine tea the whole afternoon, or ate only fruit. Such a lack of structure would have been unthinkable in Akbar Ahmad's lifetime.

For the first time since her marriage, and at her sister Hina's suggestion, Mona took up a hobby and began gardening. Mona's reminiscences of her childhood home were inseparable from the memories of the courtyard flower beds tended by her mother. Her mother had taught Mona how to plant and care for saplings. Those memories remained with Mona even after more recent events of her married life were forgotten.

The garden was one place where Mona spent money freely and of her own accord.

MONA WAS SHOCKED to find out how much money Akbar Ahmad had left behind. In her mind, she could not reconcile the amount with all those years of frugal existence and her losing battle against his arguments for balancing the income against an assortment of what he called "immediate necessities." These turned out to be compulsory deductions for the savings accounts, insurance premiums, treasury bills, and stock exchange deposit accounts. It took Mona some time to become accustomed to the idea that she had ready access to that money and no longer had to consult her conscience or ask Akbar Ahmad's permission to spend it.

Mona had the much needed repairs done to the cracking boundary wall of the house. The paved path that led through the garden into the rooms also needed fixing. Mona's bedroom and bathroom, which were above the living and drawing rooms, needed some minor repairs to the roof, too. Akbar Ahmad had kept putting off these repairs. Finally, Mona also had a separate kitchen entrance made from the garden, so that the cook and the newly hired maidservant, Noori, could conveniently go in and out of the kitchen without disturbing her in the living room.

After paying the salaries of the household staff (a gardener was paid per visit), Mona was released from accounting for every small sum spent during the month. But even a year after Akbar Ahmad's death, she could not spend money impulsively, but it happened more and more frequently that she bought something she liked—an ornamental bowl for the coffee table or new curtains for her bedroom.

One day, while shopping with her daughter Amber, Mona spent three thousand rupees on a small rosewood table with marquetry work. The furniture shop owner had told her it was the only one left and he could not guarantee that it would be there when she next visited. Amber, too, encouraged her to purchase it. After they returned home, as Amber helped her unwrap the table, Mona's gaze unconsciously travelled up to the photograph. The expression on Akbar Ahmad's face was one of shock and disbelief. Mona went out into the garden before his remonstrating looks became unbearable.

Akbar Ahmad still looked reproachfully at her when she was unable to account for an expenditure, but as time went on, his objections rang fainter and fainter.

II

THE MAN NEXT DOOR

A year after Akbar Ahmad's death, Mona was well settled in her new life. She was enjoying gardening. With the gardener's help, she had transformed the spacious lawn from a grassy desolation marked with a dozen or so potted evergreens into a luxurious stretch of rare flowers, creepers and shrubs. The morning glory slowly began to cover the walls of the summerhouse and Mona planted seasonal peonies and lilies.

The gardener dropped by one day in the evening on his way to the nursery to find out if Mona needed more marigolds for her landscaping. After he left, she sat down on the easy chair on the lawn by the summerhouse. The day had been particularly hot, though a few scattered showers in the afternoon had brought a little respite from the severe humidity, and by early evening a light, pleasant breeze had picked up. As Mona prepared to go indoors she saw day labourers on her neighbour

Mrs. Baig's balcony, which overlooked her lawn. They
were carrying in furniture and luggage. It seemed a new
tenant was moving into the upper storey of Mrs. Baig's
house. The elderly Mrs. Baig had been a family friend
long before they became neighbours. Having lost her
husband at the same age in her life as Mona recently had,
Mrs. Baig understood Mona's loneliness. For her part,
Mona had become more appreciative of Mrs. Baig's sense
of purpose in the face of her solitude. Mrs. Baig had been
a social worker since her university days, and remained
quite active even now, though she was fifteen years older
than Mona. The diminutive Mrs. Baig in her sari and flip-
flops was a familiar sight when heckling and exhorting
staff at the offices of local councillors and the utility services boards. Now that she was free from household routines, Mona sometimes accompanied her there. Mainly
on account of Mrs. Baig's efforts, utility services were not
as frequently disrupted in their neighbourhood as in the
rest of the city.

The modest upper portion of Mrs. Baig's house had
two small rooms, which she had recently decided to rent
after her son and daughter-in-law moved out and into a
bigger house.

The following day was again humid. After lunch, as
Mona rose to turn up the fan, the bell rang. The gardener
had come to drop off the marigolds. He was in a hurry and
promised Mona he would come early the next morning
to plant them. As she closed the gate behind him Mona
noticed Mrs. Baig's new tenant standing on the balcony
and smoking a cigarette.

He was a stocky man. Although his face betrayed no certain age, she thought he was perhaps in his late fifties. He
was dressed in a tunic and waistcoat. His moustaches were
accentuated by his dyed jet-black hair, and looked comical.
Mona wondered when she would see his wife. She thought
the couple were probably by themselves, with children
married or studying in some other city.

As Mona looked on, she saw the tenant look at her, smile,
and nod meaningfully. In that unguarded moment Mona
half-nodded in response. Then, realizing the brazenness of
his gesture, her sense of dignity was deeply offended. Mona
wondered what kind of a woman he might think she was.
She was no longer even sure that she had not smiled back. If
she hadn't, at least she could have considered complaining
to Mrs. Baig—although that had its own risks. Mrs. Baig had
a loose tongue. The accusation alone would create a scandal,
and if he denied everything it would start other rumours.

Later that evening, she remembered the new neighbour's impertinent smile. The appearance and manner of
the man was vulgar, and she was surprised at his temerity.
If she had smiled back in her nervousness she would have
only herself to blame if he read any encouragement in her
response. She suddenly wondered if he could be a crimi-
nal. In her imagination the bold smile metamorphosed
into a sinister sneer. Before going to bed, she locked all the
door and windows and brought the phone close to her bed.

In the morning, she thought it was silly of her to worry.
She realized that the cautious Mrs. Baig would not let a vil-
lain into her house as a tenant. She was almost able to forget the unpleasant incident.

~~~

A FEW DAYS LATER, Mona found marigold plants lying outside the gate. The gardener had already planted those he'd bought for her earlier, so she could not understand why he had brought more.

"They're for Mrs. Baig's new tenant. I have to go there once I finish here," the gardener told her, explaining that the man had stopped him in the street the day before, and asked him for the same kind of flower the neighbour had seen planted in the house opposite. There was a nice garden in Mrs. Baig's house, but the balcony's only plant was a drab money-plant vine. The next day, when Mona went out into the garden, she saw the marigolds potted along one wall of Mrs. Baig's balcony. She realized she had become used to the sight of Mrs. Baig's son and daughter-in-law on the balcony. It had not occurred to her that her whole garden was exposed now to a stranger's view.

That afternoon after lunch, Mona went to see Mrs. Baig. She found her neighbour pouring water into the clay bowls in the budgerigars' cage that was fitted into the narrow stretch of the veranda's southern wall. Mrs. Baig did not hear her approach, probably because she was not wearing her hearing aid. When Mona repeated her greeting, Mrs. Baig turned with a start.

"Oh God, I thought someone had walked in from the street! Come inside. I'm almost finished here."

As they walked into the living room, Mona asked her about the tenant.

"No, no, there's no family," Mrs. Baig said. "He's a widower. The wife died some years ago. No children either."

Thoughts of Akbar Ahmad's death were still fresh in Mona's memory, and she felt a momentary pang of empathy upon hearing of the new neighbour's loss. Then, remembering his vulgar smile, her annoyance returned. She casually mentioned that one could not be too careful with strangers these days. Mrs. Baig told her she had taken all necessary precautions and had checked the references. The man had come well recommended, although Mrs. Baig could not tell precisely what he did for a living. He had mentioned something about a distribution agency. Mrs. Baig was not worried, because he had paid six months' rent in advance. Mrs. Baig provided no other information than his name—Salamat Ali.

ABOUT A WEEK LATER, Mona found the gardener planting rose bushes in an empty corner of her garden. He had planted two of them already and was nearly finished with the third.

"Where did these come from?" Mona asked.

"Salamat Ali ordered these rose bushes and some were left over. I'd told him not to order too many, but he didn't listen! He said to plant them somewhere else. Then we saw how barren this patch looked from there." He pointed towards Salamat Ali's balcony. "He suggested that perhaps I should plant them here."

Mona looked up and saw newly potted rose bushes slowly swaying along the eastern edge of Mrs. Baig's balcony.

"Why didn't you plant them in Mrs. Baig's garden?"

"There's no place there. It's already full."

Mona's first impulse was to stop the gardener and ask him to return the rose bushes. She felt certain that Salamat Ali had ordered extra plants deliberately. Then she reconsidered. The gardener was not conscious of any motive in Salamat Ali's suggestion to plant the rose bushes in her garden. Once before, too, he had brought some seasonal flowers and planted them without asking her. If she told him to return them, he would begin to think that there was some significance attached to Salamat Ali sending her the plants.

"I had planned to plant jasmine in that corner," she said. "You should have asked me first."

"The roses needed this shady area by the wall. Long exposure to the sun doesn't harm the jasmines. And they're not in season now. I'll bring you a batch when they are. You'll see how nicely these roses bloom. They're an expensive variety."

Salamat Ali's overture made Mona angry.

DURING THE NEXT FEW WEEKS, Mona noticed that Salamat Ali travelled to and from Mrs. Baig's house at odd hours. Other than his regular respectful nods, which she always made a point to ignore, there was for some time no further communication between them.

Mrs. Baig told her that sometimes he returned late at night, but she was happy enough with him as a tenant. Without her having to ask, he had repaired the netting of the budgerigars' cage and bought her a long-spouted watering can with which she could fill their water bowls through the bars. Mona saw why the pennywise Mrs. Baig was so pleased with Salamat Ali. Gradually Mona's apprehensions about Salamat Ali subsided. She told herself that she had overreacted to his gesture, perhaps because she felt unsafe living by herself.

Not long afterwards, the rosebuds appeared and blossomed into beautiful flowers. They were a rare and expensive variety, as the gardener had said; Mona had seen them sold in flower shops at prohibitive prices. She admired the flowers from a distance but did not go near the corner of the garden where they were planted. When the wind blew indoors, she could not tell whether the fragrance came from the flowers in her own garden or from Salamat Ali's balcony, which was crowded with them. One morning, however, Mona could not keep herself away. It was early and the garden was filled with the scent of roses. Mona looked around to make sure there was nobody on Mrs. Baig's balcony. She saw that the dew fallen overnight still lingered on the flower petals. Mona caressed them and breathed in the scent. Something revived the memory of her childhood home, where several rose bushes grew. Many years ago she and Hina had picked fresh roses for the vase kept on her mother's dresser.

Mona had plucked two flowers and was returning indoors when she sensed the presence of another person in the garden. She turned abruptly, but it proved only an illusion: she was alone. Then she noticed Salamat Ali watering the flowers on his balcony. His back was turned to her. She hurried inside the house, worried that he might have seen her plucking the roses. Was he there all along? she asked herself. Her growing anxiety seemed irrational, and she felt upset with herself for hurrying away after catching sight of him. There was no need to act like a thief on her own property.

Earlier, she had dismissed the idea of thanking Salamat Ali for the flowers because she wished to deny him the attention he seemed to crave. And it was not as if he had sent them specifically for her. As far as Mona was concerned, he had given them to the gardener. He was playing a game of pretense, and she could do the same. But now Mona reconsidered the circumstances and realized her earlier mistake. She was a middle-aged widow, not an adolescent girl, and by not acknowledging the gift she had silently conceded that there was some meaning attached to it. She had allowed a situation to develop that put her at a disadvantage. She should have spoken to him about the rose bushes. Then she could have gracefully refused any further gifts and also put him on notice against taking similar liberties in the future. Her manner gave the impression that she was timid and could be manipulated. Now that he had caught her stealing away with the roses, she must dispel that impression.

But weeks had passed since he sent the rose bushes, and Mona felt that to bring up the subject after such a long time would not serve her well in avoiding his further attentions.

~~~

THE BELL RANG LATE one afternoon, and when Mona answered, she found Salamat Ali standing there.

"These are for you," he said, thrusting a box of sweet-meats towards Mona.

"What do you mean, these are for me?" Mona said, pushing away the box. "Who do you think you are? Don't ever make such advances to me again! If you wish to live in this neighbourhood you must learn to behave yourself, and the sooner the better. God knows where people such as you come from." Mona's earlier impression of Salamat Ali, her strong sense of her widowhood, and the consciousness that she was the mother of grown-up and married daughters as well as a respected figure in the community made her furious at Salamat Ali's boldness and audacity. She was about to slam the door when he stepped aside and she saw Mrs. Baig waving at her from her gate across the street.

Salamat Ali smiled impertinently. "As I was saying, these are for you, from your neighbour, Mrs. Baig."

"My son got the promotion I was praying for, Mona!" Mrs. Baig called out from across the way. "I was too tired today to go delivering sweets around the neighbourhood myself. Poor Salamat Ali, he's been distributing them for me all afternoon."

Mona was mortified. She could not look Salamat Ali in the eye. She only hoped that Mrs. Baig was not wearing her hearing aid and had not heard her outburst. Confused and embarrassed, she looked away as she took the box of sweetmeats from his hands.

Salamat Ali put his head inside the gate and took a quick peek at the garden. "So, you liked the roses?"

"Yes . . . No . . . It wasn't proper. I mean, there was no need to send them. What I mean is, you shouldn't have done it!"

She saw that he enjoyed her discomfort.

"The poor plants would have died. I'm sure you wouldn't have wished that. I'm grateful you accepted the gift. You'll like them. Early in the morning when the dew has fallen, they give out a particularly captivating smell!"

"The next delivery is to the house with the green gate," Mrs. Baig shouted from her doorway. "Just a few trips more, Salamat Ali!"

Salamat Ali turned and hurried away.

"The cheek of the man!" Mona said to herself as she closed the gate.

Once Mona came inside the house she looked in the nearest mirror and saw that her face was flushed. She was angry with herself because she had jumped to conclusions. She had ended up looking even more ridiculous than when he had seen her hurrying inside that morning after plucking the roses.

But Mona felt a degree of satisfaction in having had the opportunity to shout at Salamat Ali, and after a few moments' reflection, decided she had in fact communicated her message. Now he knew her opinion about his behaviour. She realized there had been no visible change in his manner even after hearing her outburst. He had smiled mulishly, as if he were used to hearing abuse from women. She wondered if that was his usual manner with women. Then, recalling Salamat Ali's comic appearance, she laughed at herself for imagining him to be something of a Don Juan. Suddenly, she caught sight of her blouse in the mirror. She was embarrassed to see that the new cotton blouse had shrunk and become a little too tight after washing. What had she been thinking when she was putting it on? she wondered. In that tight blouse with her exposed cleavage, she looked like some vulgarly dressed dancer from a B-movie. She recalled how Salamat Ali had taken his peek inside the garden while she was standing at the threshold. With a growing feeling of consternation, she covered her cleavage with the folds of her sari.

Mona regarded herself in the mirror with greater attention. Better to look like a B-movie dancer, she thought, than someone like Mrs. Kazi, her daughter Tanya's mother-in-law. Though only a few years older than Mona, Mrs. Kazi looked quite haggard. Mona had always seen the jealous look of a rival in the woman's eyes. Any doubts she might have had were recently dispelled by Mrs. Kazi herself. Just a week ago, she had told Tanya she was convinced Mona dyed her hair and pretentiously left a little undyed around the temples. When later Tanya phoned her mother to tell her what Mrs. Kazi said, Mona had laughed. The strands around her temple had begun greying in the last few years but she never thought of dyeing them. Mona had thought of asking Tanya why she had not corrected her mother-in-law, but then she felt irritated and changed the subject. Mona recalled Mrs. Kazi's remark now as she looked in the mirror, and thought she did look young for her age. After her bath earlier that afternoon she had dried her hair and tied it up in a bun. Her slender neck was exposed to her shoulders, and some tendrils of hair, still wet from the bath, clung to her skin. She thought that if she did dye her hair, she could easily pass for someone in her early forties, or even late thirties. Her face had no wrinkles. The little weight she had put on around the waist was beginning to disappear from regular walking, and her torso was not bulging out even in this tight blouse.

Her gaze travelled down and she noticed small threads from the hem of the old petticoat coming out from under the folds of the sari, hanging over her feet. It made her look like someone who dressed dowdily. She suddenly felt frustrated at the direction her thoughts were taking. What girlish concerns. Who on earth cares what that idiot Salamat Ali thought of her.

More than once Mona had suspected Salamat Ali of crudely communicating his feelings to her. She found it difficult to accept, because as far as she was concerned the course of her life as a widow was now determined to the end of her days. She could neither imagine nor wish for any change in it. The idea of a stranger lurking somewhere in her life with her husband so recently dead was offensive to her. It also made her feel strangely guilty. She wondered if there was something in her demeanour that had encouraged such advances from the man. She tried to think rationally about the situation. Salamat Ali's unpolished manner aside, she asked herself, what exactly might he be hoping to achieve? He could easily find a younger woman. Unlike middle-aged women, men his age never seemed to run out of youthful prospects. Or was it companionship he sought? Was he just trying to be nice as a neighbour? She knew that anyone looking at them from an objective distance would say that he could be after her money. Was he?

She was never able to ask this last question of herself with conviction or answer it with clarity. When the thought did occur to her, she could not dwell on it for too long—not because she had any proof of Salamat Ali's true intentions, but because, until recently, she had not had any control over the money that was now all hers. The thought of her financial independence pleased her, but it did not evoke any thoughts of a required vigil over it. She had yet to develop a sense of ownership of her wealth, and her instincts were not as quick and keen on defending it, for instance, as they were in defending her sense of propriety.

All those thoughts occupied her for the rest of the day. Towards evening it began raining. She ate her dinner in the humid kitchen and, as she did so, she remembered a snatch of an old song from a movie and began humming. She was feeling restless and spent nearly half an hour cleaning the refrigerator and the kitchen cabinets. Then she gathered some magazines, made tea for herself and took everything into the living room. Suddenly she paused, changed her mind, and instead went to the bedroom.

Sitting upright in bed, she picked up the home decoration magazines she had borrowed from Mrs. Baig and flipped through the pages, but she could not focus on anything. The pattering of the rain on her windows sometimes grew louder with a change in the wind. She stayed up a good part of the night.

While her husband was alive, Mona had stayed up late only when someone in the family was sick. Akbar Ahmad always went to bed by ten o'clock, and because he was a light sleeper, even when she was unable to sleep she never turned on her bedside lamp to read for fear of waking him. If she disturbed his sleep, he did not let her forget it—even when she started from a nightmare or if a migraine made her toss restlessly in bed.

Then Mona remembered one incident when she had stayed up the whole night. Even now she felt embarrassed at the thought of it.

Some years ago, on the evening of their Silver Jubilee and after the guests had left, Mona had put away the dishes and come up to the bedroom. Akbar Ahmad was already in bed and preparing to sleep. He had put his glasses on the side table. Mona stood before the dressing table tying her hair in a bun and wrapping a string of jasmine buds around it. Akbar Ahmad asked her to switch off the light, but she ignored him. Then she walked up to the bed, turned her head around to show him her hair arrangement, and asked, "What do you think of it?"

Akbar Ahmad slowly sat up and put on his glasses. She let him admire her.

"It looks nice, Mona. You look very nice . . ."

As Akbar Ahmad hesitated, she turned to face him. He was struggling with something he wanted to say. Clearly, he had read Mona's intent. Slowly and hesitantly but with care and without looking her in the eye, he said, "There's something . . . something I've been meaning to say. We must not . . . We have grown-up daughters now. It seems improper for people of our age. Come, let's go to sleep." Then he put his glasses back on the side table, pulled up the sheets and turned his back to her.

She could not remember switching off the lights and getting into bed herself.

Now, listening to the falling rain, Mona tried but could not recall the last time they had made love.

SALAMAT ALI HAD NOT been heard from for the past few weeks. This made Mona feel confident that their last encounter had been decisive and that he would not dare to cross her path again. At first she had felt a sense of satisfaction, then wondered if she had been too harsh with him. She felt embarrassed about her outburst and exasperated at her girlish behaviour when dealing with him.

One day Mona took some leftover mince-filled potato cutlets over to Mrs. Baig. As she was about to enter the house she caught sight of Salamat Ali on the balcony. She noticed that when he saw her looking up at him, he turned away with a degree of affectation.

As Mrs. Baig was getting up to make tea for Mona, the power went off. Mrs. Baig cursed loudly. "This is the second time in three days that they've cut off the electric supply without notice. God knows how long it'll take before the electricity is restored. I put away the milk in the fridge this morning without first boiling it. It will go rotten in a few hours. What will I do for tea tomorrow morning?"

"I'll bring you some later tonight," Mona said. She found

herself wondering why Salamat Ali was suddenly acting indifferent.

"It's twenty rupees a litre now!" Mrs. Baig was saying. "Imagine! Twenty rupees for one litre of milk! It was just a year ago that I paid fifteen."

"Has there been a power failure, Mrs. Baig?" Salamat Ali called out from the staircase.

"What do you think?" Mrs. Baig said irritably. "Of course there's been a power failure."

"Is somebody there with you?" Salamat Ali asked again. "Can I come down to borrow a hand-fan if you've got an extra one?"

"You can come down," Mrs. Baig said. "There's only Mona here."

Mona expected him to come down directly, but when he didn't, she thought perhaps it was his way of conveying to her that he felt hurt. Does he expect me to apologize to him? Mona decided she would not do any such thing.

Mrs. Baig was telling Mona about her daughter-in-law's garish new hairstyle and either did not notice or did not care that Salamat Ali had not come down.

When a few more days passed and Mona did not see Salamat Ali on the balcony or around Mrs. Baig's house, she wondered if he was secretly watching her. She suspected he was. She sometimes felt his presence.

Early in the mornings, when she went out into the garden and stood before the rose bushes, she looked from the corner of her eye towards the opposite balcony, but always found it deserted. Later in the evenings, she switched off the lights of the house early to see if he was standing there.

She stood behind a curtain to make sure she could not be seen. Again she saw no sign of him. Mona was convinced that he had taken offence at her earlier behaviour.

SOME DAYS EARLIER, Amber had called Mona and made plans to go to the cinema. The old classic *Mughal-e Azam* was showing again, and only two days remained before the last screening. Mona had intended to ask Mrs. Baig, too, but Amber told her that when she and her husband, Kamal, came to pick her up from her house, they planned to leave their daughter with Mrs. Baig.

On the morning of the show, Amber phoned and told Mona that Kamal's relatives had called from out of town without notice and informed them of their arrival that day. Thus Amber had to cancel her plans for the movie. Mona replied that she would ask Mrs. Baig to come with her instead. Amber told her that Kamal's driver would drop them at the cinema on his way to the airport to pick up the visitors, and bring them home again at the end of the show.

When Mona went to Mrs. Baig's house to invite her, she found Salamat Ali sitting outside on the veranda. He was oiling locks and sorting keys for Mrs. Baig, who had collected a huge assortment of these after an incident several years ago when a robber tried to break into a neighbourhood house. Before going to bed, she still fastened ten locks on her doors.

Salamat Ali did not look up as Mona came in.

All a pretense, Mona said to herself. Look at him sitting there like a member of the family. Salamat Ali's feet were propped up on a side table. After casting a sideways glance at him, Mona went inside.

Mrs. Baig wanted to come with Mona because she had not seen *Mughal-e Azam* for many years, but her hearing aid had recently broken. She had given up social activities until a repair or replacement could be made.

By the time Mona left Mrs. Baig's house, Salamat Ali was no longer on the veranda.

THERE WAS ONLY one showing at the cinema that day and it was to end early in the evening. Mona knew it was pointless to invite Tanya, who hated old movies. Mona decided to go alone, something she had never done before. If she sat next to a family, nobody would know she had come to watch it by herself, she thought. In any event, because it was the last show—and a weekend—many families would be there and she would not be noticed. Mona had her bath, ate lunch and made tea. By the time Amber's driver arrived to pick her up, she was dressed and ready to embark on her little adventure.

After she was dropped off, Mona entered the cinema house, but soon realized she should have asked the driver to get her the ticket before he left. There were long lineups at the ticket windows. The wicket marked for families was open, but there, too, men stood in a queue and she felt too intimidated to stand among them by herself. Mona remembered how convenient it was when Akbar Ahmad was alive. They received gallery passes for every new movie. Though she mostly gave the passes to Tanya and

Amber, as Akbar Ahmad never had time for movies. Now Mona deliberated on whether to turn back or steel herself and join the lineup at the ticket window. Waiting for a taxi and haggling for fare on the busy street would be just as challenging. She did not wish to leave without watching the movie.

Suddenly, someone brushed past, almost pushing her to the side. Mona caught a glimpse of Salamat Ali's dyed hair as he disappeared through the glass door of the entrance. She was enraged at this new effrontery. Then she realized that a ticket had been pushed into her hand.

An older man standing nearby with his wife approached her.

"Are you okay?" he asked her. "Did that man push you? I'll go inside and drag him out by his collar!"

"No, no, it was an accident." Mona tried to hide the ticket stub under her purse.

The man looked at her suspiciously. To avoid further scrutiny, Mona moved towards the entrance door. As she entered the darkened theatre, as usual she felt almost blinded. She followed the usher to her seat. She was glad it was a corner seat and there was another woman sitting next to her. Mona wondered if Salamat Ali was watching her still. She remained conscious of his presence throughout, and, as a result, was unable to concentrate on the movie.

When the lights came on during the intermission, someone behind her reached over and put a bottle of Fanta in her hand.

"Please take it." She heard Salamat Ali's whisper.

She dared not refuse; someone might notice.

When the film continued, Mona could not concentrate. She kept feeling Salamat Ali's gaze on the back of her neck. At the end of the show she got up and left without looking back.

Amber's driver was waiting outside the theatre. As she climbed into the car, she saw no sign of Salamat Ali outside the cinema.

A little while after she returned home, she heard a taxi stop in the street outside. She waited a few moments for the taxi to leave before peeking out of her bedroom window. She saw the light come on in Salamat Ali's room.

A FEW DAYS AFTER her visit to the cinema, Mona made *ras-malai*. She did not have a sweet tooth generally, and was fond only of the *ras-malai* her mother used to make when they had guests. Mona had learned the recipe just from watching her. Mrs. Baig, who also liked it, had asked her recently when she would next make some.

Mona filled a bowl with *ras-malai* to take to Mrs. Baig. As she was stepping out of her gate, she saw Salamat Ali leave the house. At the same moment she heard her phone ring and went back inside to answer the call. As she came in through the kitchen, she put the dessert in the fridge. She wondered if Salamat Ali thought that she had turned back upon catching sight of him.

After talking to Amber on the phone, Mona forgot all about the dessert, and by the time she remembered, it was already past Mrs. Baig's lunchtime. Mona decided to take the dessert over so that Mrs. Baig could have it with her evening tea or dinner.

Mrs. Baig's gate was locked, and even after Mona rang twice, nobody answered. She wondered if Mrs. Baig could not hear the bell because she was not wearing her hearing aid. Mona turned to go back, but a moment later heard the gate open. It was Salamat Ali.

She realized he must have returned to Mrs. Baig's while she was talking on the phone. She felt confused. She remembered she had not thanked him for the cinema ticket and did not know how to do so without sounding awkward.

"I did not get a chance to thank you for the cinema—" she said.

"Oh no, no, no!" He smiled as he extended his hand and took the bowl of *ras-malai* from Mona. "I was only doing my duty as a neighbour. You did not have to do all this. What *is* it?" He removed the lid of the bowl and looked inside.

Mona realized with horror that he had misunderstood. "This is not—" She stopped. How could she tell him that the sweetmeat was not meant for him? She panicked. "Ah, *ras-malai*! My favourite," he said. "Don't say this is nothing. It looks homemade. You must have made it with your own hands. Thank you so much. You shouldn't have. You embarrass me. What I did was nothing. I am glad you enjoyed the movie. That was all I cared about, really."

Mona knew that she had blundered yet again, but did not know how to fix the situation. She did not wish to offend him. She realized that if only she had thought about bringing a portion for him as well, her gesture could not have been misconstrued.

"I will make sure to share the *ras-malai* with Mrs. Baig," Salamat Ali said.

"What?" Mona asked. "No! No!"

"Why not?" Salamat Ali asked innocently.

Mona realized that if he did so it would create a small disaster. In addition to whatever Mrs. Baig might think about her secret dealings with Salamat Ali, she would take offence that Mona had brought something for her tenant and not for her. This would not do.

"I will bring another portion for Mrs. Baig!" she said hastily, then turned and started back across the street. As she did so she realized that now she had implied that the *ras-malai* was indeed meant for Salamat Ali.

"And how did you find out I like *ras-malai* so much?" Salamat Ali called out as she was walking away. "You must have asked Mrs. Baig."

Mona had not realized that there was very little *ras-malai* left at home. She could not take that small portion to Mrs. Baig. She decided to buy some for Mrs. Baig from the sweetmeat vendor.

Walking towards the sweetmeat vendor located a few blocks down the street near Tariq Road, Mona continued to feel vexed with herself. What infuriated her even more was that she could not tell whether this latest was a genuine misunderstanding, or Salamat Ali had again played a trick on her.

If it was indeed a misunderstanding, she feared that Salamat Ali would feel that he was being encouraged. She would have nobody but herself to blame.

And if it was a trick . . .

Mona did not want to think about the possibility.

She felt thankful when, on her return with the store-bought dessert, Mrs. Baig answered her own door.

III

THE LETTER

When Mona met Mrs. Baig for an evening walk some weeks later, she thought her neighbour looked at her strangely. Mrs. Baig kept staring at her. Mona thought perhaps Mrs. Baig's new hearing aid was not properly adjusted and that she was having difficulty listening to her without following her lip movement.

In the park Mrs. Baig told Mona how useful Salamat Ali had been around the house in the months that he had lived there and about all the help he offered her without being obliged to do so. "After all, he's just a tenant and owes me nothing besides the rent. But what a nice man! He comes and helps me with every small thing. His wife, poor woman, must have been very lucky. Our men don't move even to get a glass of water for themselves. The wives have to run errands for them morning to night."

Mona smiled. Akbar Ahmad had never helped her with any household chores. Mona had become so used to her leisure now that she often wondered how she did so much work during Akbar Ahmad's lifetime.

"He had no children and for a long time he felt too heartbroken to think of another woman," Mrs. Baig was saying. "I asked him why he didn't marry again."

Mona wondered what had come over Mrs. Baig. It was one thing to exchange the usual gossip about someone living in the same house, but in this instance she felt Mrs. Baig had some purpose in addressing the information specifically to her. This made Mona uneasy.

"He told me that for one reason or another he didn't feel like accepting any matches friends asked him to consider. But that was some time ago. He feels lonely now. I can tell. Let's sit down on that bench there."

They seated themselves, and Mona listened quietly as Mrs. Baig continued.

"He has a thriving paper distribution agency. He's been in the trade for many years now, you see. But you know how they say money alone can't buy happiness and peace. He told me he had to sell his house because living alone for a year after his wife's death was beginning to drive him crazy."

Mrs. Baig was staring at Mona again.

"It hasn't rained this whole month. I guess the monsoons are over," Mona said.

Mrs. Baig seemed not to have heard her remark.

"Mona," she said almost in a whisper. "Do you feel lonely sometimes?"

Mona turned abruptly to look at her, then lowered her gaze. "Why do you ask?"

"No reason, I was just thinking it must be difficult for you being all alone in the house." Mrs. Baig now fixed her eyes on the grassy patch in front of the bench. "When Akbar Ahmad was alive, there was always someone coming or going. Now you're there by yourself. And you're still young. Not old and decrepit like me."

"Nobody could say you are old and decrepit, Mrs. Baig. You are more active than many young people."

Mrs. Baig smiled complacently.

"As for me, I've gotten used to being alone in the house. It was not as difficult as I had first thought. The girls drop in every now and then."

"I never said it to you, Mona, but in my own case, my son's presence in the house lessened my sense of loneliness and was a diversion. Your daughters were already married when Akbar Ahmad died."

"They never let me feel that they've left."

"Yes, your daughters are wonderful. Much better than my son. Humph! Look at him! After living here for five years he takes off all of a sudden and now drops by only once a month. I don't demand that he visit me every week. But doesn't he live in the same city? A visit once a fortnight isn't too much to ask, is it?"

Mona felt glad of the change of subject. That of her daughter-in-law was a sore one for Mrs. Baig. While her son and daughter-in-law were living with her neighbour, Mona had tried several times to advise her against interfering in their daily lives, but Mrs. Baig could not accept the independence of her son's household. That her son should defer to his wife's opinion in daily matters was too

much for her to bear. One day the daughter-in-law had had
enough, and insisted the couple move to a rented house far
away from Mrs. Baig's neighbourhood. For the rest of the
evening they talked about Mrs. Baig's son and her
daughter-in-law. The discussion continued through their
dinner together, until Mona took her leave around eight
o'clock. Mrs. Baig saw her to the door. Mona noticed that an
anxious look had returned to Mrs. Baig's face. As she
walked away, even with her back turned Mona felt Mrs.
Baig staring at her.

LATE NEXT EVENING, Mona heard someone ring the bell. She
answered and found an agitated Mrs. Baig standing outside.

"Is everything okay, Mrs. Baig?" she asked.

Mrs. Baig nodded meaningfully as she stepped inside.

"Please tell me, what is the matter?" Mona asked, after
she had ushered her neighbour into the living room. Mrs.
Baig sat down but looked anxiously at Mona.

"It's about Salamat Ali," she finally said.

"What has happened?" A nameless anxiety gripped
Mona's heart. "Should I—Should I call the police?"

"Don't be so crazy!" Mrs. Baig suddenly chuckled.

Mona looked at Mrs. Baig's face without smiling. She
was not relieved by the change in her manner.

"What is it?" Mona asked, glancing at the envelope that
Mrs. Baig withdrew from under the folds of her sari and
placed on a table.

"What it is, you'll read yourself," Mrs. Baig said, and
promptly got up.

They walked together to the gate. "You're like a daughter to me, Mona," Mrs. Baig told her. "Do think carefully before you make a decision. I want you to be happy."

Mona closed the gate behind her neighbour and returned to the living room.

The envelope stared at her from the table.

Mona picked up the envelope and turned it over in her hands for a few moments. Then slowly she took out the letter, unfolded it and, without sitting down, read it.

Respectable Mrs. Mona Akbar Ahmad,

Please excuse me for addressing you directly. We have been neighbours for a little over six months now. On many occasions I have sincerely regretted the times when you found my behaviour and manner objection-able, and I ask your forgiveness for those times.

Mrs. Baig has kindly consented to deliver this letter for me. Because she is your friend and a well-wisher, I have already shared the contents of this letter with her. I also explained to her the few misunderstandings that caused your earlier displeasure. I assure you that I admire and respect you greatly.

Not too long ago, I also lost someone with whom I had spent a good part of my life. Until recently I had avoided even the thought of sharing my life with another person. Therefore, I can understand how you might feel. But ever since I saw you, I have constantly thought that a life with you would be full of joy and contentment.

With an earnest hope that you will not refuse me, I would like to ask for your hand in marriage. I do not wish you to answer in a hurry. I know you will have many things to consider. It had occurred to me that my proposal should have been sent through your family elders. However, I decided that I should ask your opinion first. I will be more than willing to contact your family when you advise me to do so. I hope to be able to satisfy any scrutiny into my personal affairs. I can also provide satisfactory evidence that I am able to support a household which meets your standard of living.

    I promise to make our union as happy as possible. I am sure we will find happiness and our married life will be as pleasurable for you as any man could hope to make it for a woman he truly loves.

    Yours with sincere regards,
    Salamat Ali

Mona sat down with a sense of relief. She was tired of the charade. With the letter, matters had now come to a pass where she must act decisively to put the whole thing behind her once and for all. She recalled the *ras-malai* incident and realized that her fear had been justified: Salamat Ali had felt encouraged by it. She was grateful, however, that Salamat Ali had not attempted anything scandalous. Receiving a marriage proposal through a trusted friend could invite no gossip about her.

When she retired to bed Mona took the letter with her and read it once again. Salamat Ali's handwriting—like a child's—flowed unevenly on the unlined paper and dropped off towards the edge.

IV

THE FAMILY

Early the next morning, as she was making tea, Mona received a call from her uncle, Sajid Mir. He was the only surviving sibling of Mona's father; as their guardian he had taken in Mona and her sister after their father's death. Sajid Mir asked Mona how she was coping with her life and if she needed assistance with anything. Mona was in the midst of telling him about her daily routines when he interrupted her and asked if he could visit her sometime that week.

"Of course you can!" Mona said, although she was surprised. Sajid Mir suffered from arthritis and left his house only when there was a wedding or death in the family. "You must have dinner here. Bring Aunt Aneesa too. I'll also invite Mrs. Baig. Just last evening she mentioned your name."

"Hmm," Sajid Mir said. "Today I'm not feeling too well, and I don't know about tomorrow, either. But if I feel better I'll try to come on Wednesday, around seven o'clock. Aneesa will probably accompany me. We'll see about Mrs. Baig."

Mona did not wish to ask him the reason for his visit, but something about the early morning phone call puzzled her. Sajid Mir had studied with Mrs. Baig at the university and was always happy to see her. He had introduced the families when Akbar Ahmad and Mona moved to the neighbourhood. Why did he respond in such an offhand manner when she mentioned Mrs. Baig? Mona wondered. Did they have a fight? But when? And what about?

"Mona!" Mrs. Baig came in through the kitchen door, looking like she had not slept all night.

"I thought you should know, Mona. After visiting you last night, I was feeling confused. I didn't know if I'd done the right thing. So I called Sajid Mir to discuss the matter with him. At first he didn't understand. Then he became angry. Men are so unreasonable. Now I think I shouldn't have told him without waiting to hear your answer, but after bringing you the letter I was feeling too anxious about what I'd done. You know . . ." Mrs. Baig was out of breath.

Mona now understood the reason for Sajid Mir's call. "I just spoke to him over the phone."

"You mean with Sajid Mir?" Mrs. Baig asked.

Mona nodded.

Mrs. Baig was becoming flustered again. "So he already called, did he? Was he upset? I hope you won't hold it against me, Mona. I was too worried. It was all too much for me."

"It's all right, Mrs. Baig! What's done is done. He's coming on Wednesday to talk to me. At least now I know what it's about. What else did he say to you?"

"Nothing much, except that I had no right to do what I did. Mona, do you want me to be here when he comes? I will, if you want me to. I feel so guilty!"

"I got the impression he wanted to see me alone. If I feel he should speak to you, I'll certainly call you. And you mustn't feel guilty about anything. He had no right to speak to you in that manner."

Mrs. Baig finally felt relieved enough to sit down. Mona made tea for her. Her maidservant Noori had arrived by then, and Mona made a gesture to Mrs. Baig not to discuss the subject before her. Apparently it was not easy for Mrs. Baig to desist from it. She tried to continue talking in whispers. Her secretive manner was all too conspicuous, and intrigued Noori who began looking at them hard to figure out what was happening. Mona had to send Mrs. Baig away with the promise that she would come over to her house to talk about it later in the day.

"Did you think about the answer you want to give Salamat Ali?" Mrs. Baig asked before stepping out of the gate, almost immediately adding, "I'm sorry! I shouldn't be discussing it right now. But do come by later today. And make sure to call me tomorrow evening. Even if it's late. I'll be awake. Promise?"

Mona nodded and closed the gate behind her neighbour.

Inside, she suddenly felt weak. She collapsed onto the living room sofa. Akbar Ahmad looked down a little sternly at her, as if inquiring what all that commotion was about.

Sitting there, gazing at the portrait, Mona experienced a familiar sense of security in Akbar Ahmad's presence. Yet she was exhausted, so she decided to defer writing her reply to Salamat Ali. She did not visit Mrs. Baig either.

IN THE AFTERNOON, Amber called to tell her mother that she would be coming over shortly, and soon after that, the phone rang again. Tanya was coming over too. She told Mona that she would be leaving work early that day and that she knew Amber would be there. She said that she would pick up some Chinese food on the way. Mona wondered if they had heard something. More than anything else, she was concerned that the news not be communicated to them in a manner that would embarrass them or lead them to make wrong assumptions. It was important that she be the one who broke the news to them. She felt embarrassed at the thought of bringing up the subject of the marriage proposal.

THE LOOK ON HER DAUGHTERS' faces told Mona that she was too late.

Tanya quietly handed over the food to Mona, who had taken out the cutlery and crockery. Tanya was wearing a dark office suit. Mona noticed she had touched up her makeup before leaving the office. Amber seldom dressed up or wore makeup unless she accompanied Kamal. That day, as well, she was without any makeup and plainly dressed in a light-blue cotton shalwar-qameez suit.

Mona asked them to come to the dining table.

"Aunt Aneesa called Amber to inquire if she had heard anything about your affair with a neighbour," Tanya said, throwing her handbag on the nearby sofa.

Mona looked first at Tanya, then at Amber.

A brief, uncomfortable silence followed.

Aunt Aneesa had always had a reputation for being vitriolic, and she had never truly forgiven either Mona or her sister Hina for compromising the marriage prospects of her own daughters with their presence. Until both of them had married and left Sajid Mir's house, no proposals came for Aneesa's own daughters. Rubab, her youngest, was Mona's age, still unmarried and living at home.

Mona regarded her daughters as they sat quietly, looking expectantly at her. She was reminded of their childhood days when Akbar Ahmad was away in Islamabad and the three of them would gather around the dining table to talk. Mona became aware at that moment that the innocence of their mother–daughter relationship was tenuous.

She finally broke the silence, and briefly told the girls about the letter and her conversations with Mrs. Baig. She felt self-conscious talking to her daughters about Salamat Ali's proposal, but they showed no signs of embarrassment as they listened to her account. The generation gap between her and her daughters—both in their late twenties—had never become more apparent to her.

"What are you going to do?" Tanya asked petulantly.

"What do you mean?" Mona said sharply. Tanya's tone had nettled her and reminded her of Akbar Ahmad, of whom her daughter was a true copy. She had the same heavy chin, and like him she was a little on the heavy side. In her dark office suit, she suddenly seemed overbearing.

Before Tanya could speak, Amber interjected, "When is Aunt Hina returning?"

"She comes back in three days. I have to go and see her."

"I'll take you to her house when she returns," Tanya offered.

"No! I want to speak to her alone," Mona said, then changed the subject. "Let's eat."

Tanya sat across the table from Mona and slowly tapped the table mat with a spoon. "You still haven't told us who is this Salamat Ali," she stated impatiently.

"He's some businessman who rents from Mrs. Baig," Mona answered.

"Have you talked to him?" Tanya looked searchingly at her face.

"Once or twice, only as neighbours."

Tanya continued her interrogation. "Why did you never mention him before?"

Amber stopped emptying the rice into the serving dish.

"There was no need!" Mona said to Tanya, whose tone was beginning to irk her.

The three were suddenly silent.

"What does he look like?" Amber asked. "Wait! Don't tell me. I'll go and see for myself. I'll pretend that I've come to see Mrs. Baig." She began drying her hands.

"Where are you going?" Tanya said. "Okay. Wait. I'm also coming."

"He might not be there now," Mona called out. "Have your food first. It'll get cold."

But the girls rushed out.

Suddenly Mona thought her daughters might form an unfavourable opinion of Salamat Ali from his appearance. She hoped he was away.

Her daughters returned half an hour later.

"Salamat Ali himself opened the door for us," Amber said. "He immediately told us that we looked exactly like you and he could recognize us as your daughters without any introduction."

Mona smiled to herself at Salamat Ali's efforts to ingratiate himself with her daughters. Only Amber had inherited Mona's figure and her narrow mouth and delicate chin.

"After letting us inside, he knocked on Mrs. Baig's bedroom door a few times. We could hear her snoring loudly. She must have slept badly last night. Tanya wanted to leave then, but he insisted on making tea for us."

"He talks too much," Tanya said. "Nosy too."

"Yes, he did most of the talking, asking us what we did and where we worked. He also knew someone in Tanya's advertising agency."

"Only a junior sales executive," Tanya commented. "Nobody important. He bought some paper products from Salamat Ali for a marketing campaign."

Amber was imitating Salamat Ali's manner of waving his arms in the air when talking. She had similarly mimicked Akbar Ahmad when he was alive, although she never did it in front of him. Amber laughed, but Tanya's face became grave.

"Stop laughing!" Tanya snapped. "Didn't you see how he was flirting with you?"

"He wasn't. Don't be crazy." Amber replied, still laughing. "He only said that I sound like Mummy. What's wrong with that? It's not the first time that somebody has said it."

"That's not what he said. His exact words were, 'Your voice is as melodious as your mother's.'"

"That's the same thing!"

"No, it isn't. I didn't like his sleazy manner."

"That's your problem. I saw nothing wrong with it." Mona had been uneasy earlier, but she now relaxed. Still, she didn't like discussing the matter of Salamat Ali's proposal. She remained silent and let the girls do most of the talking.

Mona could feel her daughters' reticence. She knew that even Tanya with her brash manner had not spoken all that might be on her mind. Mona felt her own reserve towards her daughters as well. She could never have imagined that her relationship with Tanya and Amber could become so complex all of a sudden. After a while, her daughters seemed to sense that she wanted to be alone. Mona did not answer when Tanya asked her when they could go for their next shopping trip together. The girls left shortly afterwards.

Their casual discussion of the characteristics of a man who had shown interest in their mother had seemed unreal to her. Apparently, they were not as shocked about the proposal from Salamat Ali as she had expected. Even if they did not approve of the proposal itself, they saw her as someone eligible to receive one. She realized that her daughters' image of her was quite different from her own.

Mona recalled Tanya's question: *What are you going*

to do? The hostility in her daughter's voice was too obvious for Mona to ignore. Amber had noticed it, too, and turned to look at Tanya. Something had kept Mona from discussing the issue further with her daughters.

THE NEXT MORNING, Aunt Aneesa called Mona to tell her that she and her elder daughter, Rubab, would accompany Sajid Mir to Mona's house.

"He has difficulty getting in and out of the car because of his arthritis. Rubab helps him with it. I'm now too old to support him. You've stopped visiting us. I haven't seen you in such a long time. Just the other day we were talking about you! At the last family gathering you—"

"I look forward to seeing you and the family on Wednesday, Aunt Aneesa. I was just about to go out when you called. I'm rushing now. Goodbye!" Mona had no wish to hold an extended conversation with her aunt. She had not forgiven Aunt Aneesa's phone call to Amber.

SAJID MIR LOOKED PREOCCUPIED on Wednesday when he arrived. Mona was most struck by the deterioration in his physical condition. He looked worse than six months earlier when she had last seen him. His back had become bent, too. With some difficulty Rubab and the driver helped him out of the car. As usual, when Rubab greeted her, Mona had to strain her ears to make sense of her cousin's mumbling speech. Rubab had put on more weight and the seams of her embroidered pink dress were bulging. Aunt Aneesa was dressed in a drab green shalwar-qameez suit that also seemed fully inflated. Mother and daughter wore the same strong perfume, which always reminded Mona of her stay at Sajid Mir's house.

Mona soon served tea. Aunt Aneesa asked Mona about Tanya and Amber. Mona noticed that she kept looking towards Sajid Mir every few moments. A little later, Aunt Aneesa told Mona that she and Rubab would leave her with Sajid Mir while they visited Mrs. Baig, whom they had not seen in a long time. Mona felt relieved because she had been dreading an interrogation by her aunt. Mona did not know how she would keep her anger in check if another snide remark was made about her.

"I just need to use the bathroom," Rubab said.

After Rubab left, Sajid Mir sat up with effort and loudly cleared his throat. He avoided looking at Mona's face when speaking.

"You've always been my favourite niece, Mona. Your sister Hina was also close to my heart but she was a little too strong-willed for a girl. When your father died, Aneesa and I didn't hesitate even for a second in taking you into our home. And God bless both of you, neither you nor Hina ever gave us cause to regret our trust and confidence. I was so happy for you when you were married to Akbar Ahmad—an ideal man and an ideal husband. It was a great tragedy that he had to leave us all of a sudden. But thank God, you don't want for anything now. God has given you every convenience you can ask for. You are happy and you're respected throughout the family. That is the most valuable thing for a woman in the whole world and you mustn't let it be compromised."

Here Sajid Mir paused for a moment and lowered his voice. "I'd never have guessed Mrs. Baig capable of acting in such a ridiculous manner. How could she, God forbid, even think of these things? Your husband has just died. You're well-aged with two married daughters, who have, God be praised, children of their own. Mrs. Baig was very sensible once, but nerves and sanity don't last forever. What she's done is unforgivable. May God save us. I felt so embarrassed when I heard about it. I felt guilty, too, because I introduced your family to her. How could I have known I'd be faced with these circumstances one day? What a scandal it would create if someone got wind of this sordid affair. God forbid, I don't expect you to behave at all indiscreetly but I thought I should come here in person to tell you that we're with you in this hour when you've been embarrassed in this manner. And you must also take care not to breathe even a word of this story to anyone—no matter how good a friend you consider that person—otherwise we might never be able to show our faces anywhere."

Sajid Mir finally turned to face her.

Now Mona looked away. She remained quiet.

"At least say something, Mona." Sajid Mir finally said.

"I'm listening to you," Mona replied.

At that moment Sajid Mir noticed Akbar Ahmad's photograph on the wall. "Er, I didn't see this before. Looks quite real."

Perhaps noticing its presence in the house reassured Sajid Mir and had a calming effect on his nerves. He was visibly less upset than before, although Mona had not offered a proper reply.

Mona wondered if Sajid Mir would refuse to marry off Rubab if a proposal were to come for her even now. Then she wondered what Sajid Mir might have done if Aunt Aneesa had died twenty-five years ago. Would he have become celibate? He was in poor shape now, but until fairly recently Aunt Aneesa had been very distressed about his frequent out-of-town trips. There had been rumours, too, among his co-workers, of Sajid Mir's affair with his secretary.

After another tirade against Mrs. Baig's corrupt judgment and a short commentary on the opportunism of men, his mind finally wandered and he began to talk to Mona about his arthritis.

Aunt Aneesa and Rubab returned a while later.

"Are you two finished?" she asked Sajid Mir.

"Yes, yes," Sajid Mir replied.

"All is taken care of and settled?" Aunt Aneesa asked with a complacent smile.

Mona saw Rubab smile.

"Our Mona isn't stupid," Sajid Mir said. "She understands everything. I told her that all manner of opportunists lie in wait for women who have lost their husbands and have some money to their name. They lay in with honeyed words and the foolish women begin seeing green pastures. The newspapers are full of stories of women who wager their dignity and honour for such men and are killed in cold blood and disappear forever, or worse, carry their shame for the rest of their lives."

"We never made any difference between you and Hina and our own daughters," Aunt Aneesa said. "For us the two of you were the same as Rubab or her sister. And once the girls of our family are married, they leave their houses only upon their death. And look, it's not as if you're some spring chicken."

"That is exactly what I was telling Mona just now," Sajid Mir put in.

"I was so surprised that Mrs. Baig showed no regard for your advanced age or your white hair," Aunt Aneesa continued. "I always told your uncle that Mrs. Baig had a screw loose. Now at least she can blame it on her dotage. But what excuse did she have for her behaviour when she was at the university? I'll tell you all about her escapades someday."

Mona could not hold back any longer. "Mrs. Baig is my friend!" she said. "I don't wish to hear any stories about her or anybody else. And please be careful with your words when you speak to my daughters."

"Ha! Listen to this!" Aunt Aneesa shouted. "What have I done now?"

Rubab, who had been smiling to herself and munching on a handful of peanut mix, suddenly froze.

"What is all that you are talking about?" Sajid Mir demanded of Mona. "What's all this about?"

Mona now felt sure that he knew nothing of Aunt Aneesa's call to Amber. She believed Sajid Mir would never approve of Aunt Aneesa maligning her before her daughters.

"Aunt Aneesa is sitting right in front of you," Mona said. "You can ask her the details of her phone call to Amber today."

"Mona thinks I have become her enemy just because I tried to make her family see some sense." Aunt Aneesa's eyes welled up with tears. "She'll be the ruin of our family."

Sajid Mir sat for a moment with a blank expression.

"Everyone who hears of it will spit on us!" he suddenly thundered. "They won't understand that this man—what's his name—"

"Salamat Ali!" Aunt Aneesa said, after wiping away a tear with a corner of her dupatta. "—yes, this Salamat Ali is a scoundrel. They'll think that there was something in our niece's behaviour or conduct that encouraged him to take matters to this extreme. And a neighbour to boot. How the rumours will fly."

"Your uncle was going to ask his friend, a retired police chief, to have the man investigated," Aunt Aneesa said, "and to send him a warning never again to approach our niece. But I stopped him because if the word had gotten out it would have brought shame upon the whole family."

Mona was enraged. "Before you considered these matters, did you ever think of consulting me?"

"See!" Aunt Aneesa turned towards Sajid Mir. "She's telling us that she is going to marry this man."

"I'm not saying anything! I'm just telling you I can manage my affairs on my own."

Aunt Aneesa immediately changed her tone. "This is exactly what I was telling your uncle. Our Mona can manage her affairs very well on her own. So, Mona, you aren't interested in marrying this Salamat Ali? I'm just asking because I want to know your intentions."

"It's none of your business!" Mona snapped.

"There's no need to get all worked up about it," Aunt Aneesa was looking hard at Mona. "I just want to know whether or not you intend to marry this lout so that we can decide whether or not we wish to continue calling you a part of our family."

"Please do what you wish, but don't call anyone names in my house or tell me what to do." Mona said.

"Yes, of course, now you have *your* house! But I haven't forgotten the day when your uncle and I took you and your sister—orphans both of you—into *our* house. Nor have I forgotten the day when you were married from *our* house."

"I'm grateful to both of you," Mona said. "Neither I nor Hina have forgotten your kindness. But now I don't wish to hear any more on this subject. It concerns me alone."

"Aneesa, let her be," Sajid Mir said. "Just tell her that if our family honour is sullied by her actions, I'll renounce her as my niece and forbid her from even attending my funeral."

"Rubab and I are your witnesses," Aunt Aneesa said with a martyr's resolve, just as Habib entered the room to announce that dinner was served. In his anger Sajid Mir stood up unaided, went straight to the dining room and pulled out a chair. He grabbed a serving spoon and began hunting for a chicken leg in the curry bowl. Aunt Aneesa's appetite was similarly unaffected by her bilious humour. When Rubab saw that Mona did not seem upset with her, she, too, began helping herself freely to the food.

The rest of the evening passed without incident. Mona ignored the earlier unpleasantness and made a few unsuccessful attempts to engage Rubab in conversation. Rubab just kept smiling quietly to herself. From habit, Sajid Mir had begun complaining to Aunt Aneesa that because of his condition, he could not even break a piece of meat between his fingers any more. She snatched it from his hands and put it on Rubab's plate.

"There!" she said.

Sajid Mir became very quiet. Rubab carried on eating unperturbed. Mona felt grateful that Aunt Aneesa did not bring up her constipation problems until dinner was over.

APPARENTLY MRS. BAIG had been watching Mona's gate. She began ringing her bell immediately after Sajid Mir's family left.

"I remembered my promise, Mrs. Baig, and I thought of calling you, but it was too late and I decided to talk to you tomorrow morning."

"No, I must speak to you now. You'd never believe what happened."

"Something happened? What?"

"No, first tell me what Sajid Mir had to say."

"He was all determined to have Salamat Ali arrested for sending the proposal. Aunt Aneesa very kindly kept him from it. They might attempt it yet for all I know."

"I wouldn't put it beyond that woman, your Aunt Aneesa. My God, I never knew such a witch!"

"Don't worry, Mrs. Baig. She said things about me to Amber as well. I've forgiven her because of her age. She's no longer in her right mind."

"Let me tell you something, Mona. That woman is not demented. She has more cunning in her little finger than a hundred of you put together."

Mrs. Baig looked so troubled that Mona could not hold back her laughter. Mrs. Baig clearly was offended.

"I'm sorry, Mrs. Baig," Mona said. "I was just laughing at the way you're making it all sound so dramatic."

"Wait till you hear! But first give me a glass of water."

Mona brought her the water and the two sat down on the living room sofa. The glass of water did not fully calm Mrs. Baig. She kept nervously twisting the edge of her sari between her fingers.

"I told you that I'd remain home this evening," Mrs. Baig began. "I decided to take a nap, because after talking to you I realized that Sajid Mir probably would not wish to see me. Therefore, Aneesa was the last person I expected to come calling on me. I know she never liked me. When we were at university, she always pretended that I was after Sajid Mir. Not that she believed it herself. But it gave her an excuse to be nasty towards me. But what could I do? They were guests in my home. And for the first time Aneesa was behaving in a friendly manner. So, I had to show them in and offer them some hospitality."

Mrs. Baig leaned forward in a conspiratorial manner and said in a whisper, "Then, Mona, she began asking all kinds of detailed questions about Salamat Ali. And I told her the little I knew. She asked me if he was there and if I could send for him so that she could meet him. I was finally convinced that she and Sajid Mir had had a change of heart. Then Salamat Ali walked in by himself and I made the introductions."

Mrs. Baig sat up with indignation and spoke in a loud voice. "Your Aunt Aneesa—that witch—suddenly started about Rubab: what a nice girl she was, how good she was at cooking, how much she loved children, and what a wonderful wife she'd make for some lucky man one day. How she went on. God save us. What? You're laughing? This is not a joke." Mrs. Baig looked insulted.

"I'm sorry, please carry on," Mona said with a giggle.

"This woman tried to steal Salamat Ali for her idiot daughter," Mrs. Baig continued. "And isn't Rubab past child-bearing age? I couldn't believe my ears. Poor Salamat Ali! He didn't know what was going on. When Aneesa took Rubab's photograph from her purse pretending she had brought it for me to see, I finally sent Salamat Ali out of the room on the pretext of his finding my spectacles."

"There was no need to be so protective, Mrs. Baig," Mona said.

"What do you mean? How did she dare even think of such a thing when she knew I was involved. Under my own roof, too! Where was I, now? Yes, by the time Salamat Ali went out of the room, Aneesa already had all the details of what he did and where he worked and God knows what else. If I'd had the least inkling of Aneesa's intentions, I'd have flatly refused to see her. Sajid Mir will probably never speak to me again, so nothing would have been jeopardized. I thought I should let you know. I'm stupid. I should have realized something was wrong when I saw Rubab in her pink dress, wearing so much makeup in this heat. Thank God she washed it off before she left."

Mona laughed again. She remembered that Rubab had not been wearing any makeup when she arrived with Sajid Mir. She must have put it on furtively in Mona's bathroom.

And now that she thought about it, when Rubab returned from Mrs. Baig's house, her face did look as if it had been scrubbed.

As she lay down to sleep that night Mona thought about her conversation with Sajid Mir and Aunt Aneesa, recalling Rubab's antics and Aunt Aneesa's attempt to match her daughter up with Salamat Ali. In Sajid Mir's presence, Mona had felt angry and wished he would leave soon. But now she found the whole situation laughable, and she recalled a childhood incident that had left a permanent impression on her mind.

Sajid Mir's family had been visiting their house. To avoid playing with Rubab and her sister, Mona had climbed up and hidden herself in the guava tree in her garden. She found an overripe guava full of worms, and shortly after that, Rubab arrived there looking for her. On a sudden impulse, Mona hurled the guava at her. It missed Rubab, but hearing the thump and finding the fruit lying on the grass, Rubab picked it up, clearly thinking that it had fallen from the tree. Mona kept watching without doing anything to stop Rubab as she ate the guava with great relish, worms and all. Mona's lips flickered into a smile as she remembered.

SINCE RECEIVING SALAMAT ALI'S LETTER, Mona had had to contend with all the emptiness and unhappy memories of her married life. She had felt depressed. She did not wish to revisit those thirty years. She also felt unsure what to make of the letter itself.

Because she had been unable to define her relationship with Salamat Ali, she was unable to articulate her
feelings for him, even to herself. Her marriage with Akbar
Ahmad had been an arranged one, with no surprises or
unexpected twists. She could not deny that sedateness
had its advantages. Even if an illusion, it gave her a sense
of control over her destiny. She felt she had had no control over how her relationship with Salamat Ali unfolded.
Nothing in his demeanour resembled Akbar Ahmad and
therefore the image of a husband and a life partner as she
knew one. And yet, for the first time she felt a mysterious
and reckless awakening.

Mona's daughters would visit the next day. She wondered
how they felt about everything that was going on. She was
especially concerned about the effect on Tanya, who had
been very attached to Akbar Ahmad. He, too, had had a spe-
cial bond with his older daughter—until their rift over Faraz
six years before Akbar Ahmad's death. He had readily
approved Kamal's proposal for Amber, but he had been
strongly against Tanya's choice of Faraz. Although he came
from a prosperous family, he was unemployed at the time.
Mona had found herself in a quandary. Amber's in-laws had
refused to defer the marriage any longer. There was a lot of
pressure on Mona not to marry Amber first. The marriage
of a younger girl while the older was still home always
attracted the worst possible speculation about the one left
behind. Mona knew that Tanya was herself uncomfortable
about the situation. She had gathered as much from indi-
rect remarks Tanya had made to her. Amber had privately
told Mona that she did not want to have her ceremony

before Tanya's. Mona told both girls that she would not sacrifice the interests of one of her daughters over the other, and that facing idle gossip would be a small sacrifice for Tanya if she so badly wished to marry Faraz. In the end, Amber was married almost a year before Tanya. Akbar Ahmad's opposition to Faraz had been so strong that he was even willing to countenance any scandal that might be associated with Tanya. The shock of Akbar Ahmad's death had apparently erased Tanya's hostile feelings over those conflicts. Of the two girls, Tanya seemed more affected by his unexpected demise.

In recent months Mona had often thought that of her daughters, Amber was the one to whom she might be able to speak about the emptiness of her married life. She could rely on her to listen without judgment. Amber's gentle, quiet manner would allow Mona to unburden her heart freely.

Like every mother, Mona had rediscovered her daughters as married women. She had witnessed Amber reacting to many things in much the same way she did, and making many of the same mistakes she had made as a young bride. She too readily gave in to her in-laws' rather conservative interpretations of a married woman's social independence. When Mona and Hina found out that Amber's father-in-law objected to her driving alone, they decided to interfere. But Amber told them that her in-laws meant well and it was on account of her own safety that they insisted upon it. Amber had Mona's trusting side, and Mona often considered that were it not for Kamal's good nature, Amber might have ended up as unhappy as Mona—or perhaps unhappier, because Amber lacked her mother's stubborn streak. Amber's gentleness only endeared her to Mona. She was confident that Amber would not respond unreasonably to Mona's current situation.

AMBER ARRIVED a little earlier than Tanya.

"What happened with Uncle Sajid Mir?" she asked.

"He made a scene," Mona replied. "Aunt Aneesa was nasty as usual."

"She also dared to come?"

"The whole family came, even Rubab. Aunt Aneesa tried to match up Rubab with Salamat Ali when they visited Mrs. Baig."

Amber started laughing. "That woman is impossible." she said.

Afterwards, she avoided looking her mother in the eye. Mona realized she felt shy discussing the matter further. Mona changed the subject and they talked about Amber's daughter until Tanya arrived.

"That's perfect," Tanya said, when Amber told her about Aunt Aneesa's attempt to match up Rubab with Salamat Ali. Then she asked, "What did Uncle Sajid Mir have to say?"

"The usual things about the impropriety of a widow marrying. Of all the scandals it would create in the family. That I should be content and not even consider—"

"He's right. What is there to consider?" Tanya put in. "You aren't unhappy, are you?"

Mona did not reply immediately. She told herself that she must choose her words wisely to assure her daughters that she did not look upon Salamat Ali's proposal as an opportunity to settle any scores with Akbar Ahmad.

"Your father and I were not unhappy together. I want both of you to remember that always," Mona said as they sat down to lunch. "There's nothing to share that you don't already know. The last time you were here it was all so unexpected and new that I didn't know what to tell you."

"And now?" Tanya asked. "Has anything changed?" She exchanged quick glances with her sister.

"I'm still somewhat confused about the whole thing," Mona said.

"I don't know what you're doing, prolonging this circus," Tanya said. "Why didn't you say no to this man right away? Faraz will have to hear all kinds of things from his mother and family. And you already know how conservative Kamal's family is. Just think about what both of us will have to put up with if this thing is allowed to continue much longer. Tell her now." She turned towards Amber. "Tell her how Kamal's family will react."

"I told you this is all too soon," Amber protested to her sister.

Mona saw her daughter's expression change, and felt that Amber did not like Tanya's tone, though Tanya usually spoke for both of them. The relationship between her daughters reminded Mona of her own relationship with Hina, though Tanya had a mean and selfish streak, which Mona could not deny even though Tanya was her own daughter.

They ate the meal in silence.

Mona pondered the real reason for her daughters' reactions, especially Tanya's hostile attitude. She knew Tanya was not afraid of defying her in-laws and disregarding anything they said about her. Was she showing the natural reaction of a child trying to protect the image of a parent in her mind? Were her daughters acting from the jealous regard that their mother's affections should not be shared with another? She remembered Akbar Ahmad's fierce opposition to Tanya's decision to marry Faraz. Akbar Ahmad had been unable to do anything once Mona resolutely defended her daughter's right to choose what she wanted from life and live with the consequences of her decisions. However, there were two agonizing years before Akbar Ahmad gave way before her resolve. When Mona looked at Tanya, she felt that she had risked a great deal as a mother to allow her to pursue her happiness. She knew that if Tanya's marriage had failed for any reason, she would never have heard the end of it—from Akbar Ahmad, from the family and from Tanya herself.

Mona had supported Tanya's decision to marry Faraz mostly out of concern for her daughter's happiness. But on several occasions afterwards, she had realized that Tanya's decision to choose Faraz as her life partner was most astute. As with Amber, Tanya's married life had laid bare aspects of her personality that Mona did not know existed. And the more Mona discovered her selfish nature, the greater she appreciated Faraz, who put up with her frequent emotional outbursts and mean-spiritedness. Tanya's instinct about Faraz was unerring, Mona thought, because it was borne of selfishness; it allowed her to clearly foresee where her interests lay. The thought had occurred to her a long time ago in a moment of anger, but later she realized that it was not far off the mark. Any other relationship would have ended years ago. But Faraz was still there, and was, after the birth of a son, even more devoted to his wife than he had been earlier.

As the girls waited for Mona to pack the lunch leftovers, Tanya said to Mona, "What are you confused about? It would have been different if Daddy had died young. Everyone knows it's difficult for a young woman to raise kids by herself. Everybody would have understood that you had done it for us. Now, however—"

So this is what it's all about, Mona said to herself. Wasn't I a good mother to them, a good wife to their father? Why is it necessary to prove it to the world, too? If they suddenly die, must I die, too? The thought made her feel bitter. The hurried, careless manner in which she packed the leftovers caused some of it to spill onto the countertop, but she did not notice.

Tanya saw Mona's angry expression and said, "I can come and stay with you for a few days if you are feeling too lonely."

Mona did not answer. She was getting angrier and angrier. She began to wonder what, if anything, would have changed in her life if, for example, Akbar Ahmad had died twenty years ago. She had realized since his death that even in their thirty-one years of marriage she had not grown emotionally attached to him. Their relationship had not created any deep intimacy that filled her soul, or whose absence felt like an irremediable loss. The more she pondered it, the more it appeared to her that she had had two children with a stranger—and now the stranger was gone.

Mona did not even bother to come to the gate to close it when the girls left.

Suddenly Mona was no longer concerned about what her daughters thought. She felt annoyed by their manner, which suggested that they had a right over her life. She had no obligation to obtain anyone's approval or consent for something that concerned only her.

Mona wondered why Tanya, who had nothing to lose herself, resented her mother's right to make her own decisions. She could not help comparing it with her own struggle on Tanya's behalf to overcome Akbar Ahmad's objections, but she felt guilty equating her duty as a mother with her daughter's reaction. She herself had no right to expect understanding from Tanya, who perhaps felt that her actions had betrayed her father's memory.

Later, it occurred to Mona that perhaps she was not looking at the situation from her daughters' viewpoint. She had always protected them by presenting a certain image of her relationship with Akbar Ahmad. By the time Tanya and Amber could have formed an idea of her emotional relationship with their father, they were themselves married and too occupied with their own family affairs to develop an empathetic understanding of her situation. Mona had never confided in them. She did not wish them to undergo any emotional trauma that might strain their relationship with their father while he was alive. She particularly did not wish to stoke any resentment that might linger in Tanya's heart against Akbar Ahmad. Hina had often told Mona that once her daughters grew up she would be unwise to keep them out of her silent, private struggle with her relationship with Akbar Ahmad. Mona had ignored that advice. Perhaps, she thought, she herself was to blame after all for her daughters not having a true understanding of her relationship with their father.

WHEN MONA ARRIVED at Hina's house, she was greeted at the door by her brother-in-law, Jafar, who was stepping out for a business meeting.

Before leaving he said to Mona, "I'll get Hina to tell me later what all the excitement is about. I can't wait to hear all about it." Hina had come out by then and she took Mona inside.

"Couldn't you have sent for me?" Hina said, after she had heard Mona's account and read Salamat Ali's letter. "If you had called me—"

"I considered it but there was no hurry." Mona tucked a loose strand of hair behind her ear. "I didn't wish you to cut short your visit."

"No, you should have at least phoned me. Jafar could have managed without me for a day. He just needs someone to remind him to take his pills every morning."

After informing Hina about her discussions with her daughters and their reactions, Mona finally asked, "What do you think of it?"

"I think we've needed some excitement like this in the family for a long time," Hina said. "But it's not quite the scandal everyone is trying to make of it. Now, if you had eloped with him—"

"Don't talk nonsense. I asked you a question."

"How about you? What do *you* think?"

"I am still thinking," Mona said.

Hina cast a long, searching glance at Mona, who was sitting upright, watching her, looking both sad and ill at ease. Hina remained silent. She walked over to the windowsill to rearrange the crystal vases.

Mona got up and poured herself some tea.

"As you know, I didn't like Akbar Ahmad." Hina spoke with her back to Mona. "Not because of his family background, as you always thought, but because of his treatment of you. Today you'll hear me out. You always cut me off whenever I tried to discuss this with you in the past."

Hina turned to face her and regarded Mona for a moment. Mona's expression was conciliatory. Hina continued.

"His behaviour was disgraceful. You pretended that it was otherwise, but I wasn't blind. If your daughters had not been married at a young age and had stayed with you a while longer, they would have told you as much. You always maintained that he was a good father, but I always told you and I'll say it again today, so what if he was a good father? How does that redeem him if he was a bad husband? You were the one he married and made his life partner. The girls were his own flesh and blood! Even animals take care of their young. But you chose what you chose. And then, Akbar Ahmad did you the single greatest favour of his life and dropped dead. It was the best gift he could have given you. Just for that I've forgiven him everything."

Mona looked up. She wanted to protest, but didn't. Hina

was still watching her. Mona felt uneasy. She took a sip from the teacup and put her feet up on the sofa.

Hina observed all this silently, then went on. "Now you have your freedom and the money—which was always equally yours but which he never allowed you to touch. You're in good health. Your daughters are married and happy. You're free. You should value this freedom that has been given you. How can you even consider such a thing? It makes no sense to me. You were unwilling to divorce Akbar Ahmad to obtain your freedom, but when a twist of fate has released you from him, you're thinking—? Of what? Of walking into slavery once again with open eyes? I cannot understand you!" Hina paused.

"Look, it's going to be your decision. Think of your own interests. Just because there's a proposal doesn't mean that you have to jump at it. Give it some more time. A lot more time. It isn't as if Salamat Ali is some golden bird who will fly away or be stolen from you."

They looked at each other. Mona laughed.

"I only wish Aunt Aneesa had been as fired up when Akbar Ahmad's proposal came for you," Hina said. "Anyway, I wish her success. I remember seeing this fellow Salamat Ali shortly after he rented Mrs. Baig's house. He's not bad looking but absolutely lacking in polish. And his hair and clothes, my God! He doesn't even have a house of his own. What do you see in him to even consider his proposal? If you must marry again, at least find someone who looks a little more decent. Someone with whom you wouldn't feel ashamed to be seen. You know, when Jafar's cousin, Imad, came to visit us six months ago, he showed an interest in you. But when we went out you weren't even wearing any makeup. You acted as if it wasn't Akbar Ahmad who had died, but you."

"That architect?" Mona remembered. "That confirmed bachelor?"

"Yes. Now *that* would have been a good match. If you wish to give anything some consideration, why not him? He's moving to Karachi to open another office here."

"It's not as if he sent a proposal." Mona said, trying to end the discussion about Imad.

"Don't be a slave to Salamat Ali's proposal, Mona," Hina came and sat down next to her. "You aren't bound to it, even if your confused feelings make you feel right now that you are. I know Imad likes you. I don't tell you everything, you know! And I know he can easily be pushed into coming out of his confirmed bachelorhood. If you want him to send you a formal proposal, nothing could be more easily arranged. He's very bright, has a good family background, status, looks. There's nothing that anyone could point a finger at—"

"You are now confirming that you *are*, in fact, status conscious," Mona said.

"Whether you like it not, people will make comparisons between your past husband and your next choice. You're fully independent now, so you want someone who shows to advantage in such a comparison. Akbar Ahmad was at least presentable, if nothing else. And he had the courtesy not to dye his hair so hideously." Hina laughed. "God, I never thought I'd miss him one day."

Mona found it ironic that Akbar Ahmad seemed a

greater part of her life now than when he was alive. It was as if Salamat Ali's arrival had brought him back to assert his claim over her.

Hina saw Mona looking out of the window.

"You aren't listening, Mona, are you?"

Mona put down her tea.

"We don't even know the kind of family this Salamat Ali comes from and what his habits are like," Hina said when she did not get a reply from Mona. "If you and he were younger it wouldn't matter, but at our age every personality quirk stands out. Every small thing that one is unused to in the other person becomes annoying in no time."

"Do you know what it's like to live in the capacity of a servant-for-life to someone?" Mona asked.

"What do you mean?"

"Do you know how it is to feel that you are a life partner in name only? That everything revolves around another? Not only can you not have a life of your own but you must remain attached to another who has you in a subservient role!"

"We had had this discussion many times when Akbar Ahmad was alive. And this is exactly what I ask you to avoid, now that you have a life of your own. I do not understand you."

Mona felt she had become entangled in the arguments of her own confused reasoning. She could not confess to herself that her life was still not free of Akbar Ahmad's shadow—a shadow she secretly wished to dispel. She justified her freedom to choose a new life by bringing up her secret grievances. But she could not plainly admit to

Hina—whose advice to leave Akbar Ahmad she had con-
tinually resisted—that her unrequited desires had to do
with the scars left from her first marriage.

Mona suddenly got up. "I have to go home now."

Hina glanced up with surprise. "What's the hurry?"

"I have a headache." Mona looked away.

Hina watched her for a few moments in silence.

"Let me get the car keys," she said.

MONA WAS SILENT and pensive during the drive home. She
could not stop thinking about what Hina had said about
Akbar Ahmad. Although Hina had made her point more
vehemently than ever that day, she had said nothing new.
But the truth was becoming apparent to Mona. Unlike in
the past, she did not have to forcibly shut her eyes to a fact
just to make life more bearable: Akbar Ahmad was forever
gone from her life.

When she arrived home, she changed and made herself a cup of jasmine tea. As she entered the living room,
she saw Akbar Ahmad watching her with a curious expression. His look carried an element of scrutiny, as if he was
asking her if life with him had really been all that bad.
Mona tried to think of a truthful answer, but under his
gaze she could only think of one of Akbar Ahmad's own
favourite sayings: *Anyone who eats and sleeps daily is perfectly happy with his life.*

Mona could not say that she had suffered any physical
hardship in the performance of her household duties. They
even had the chopper and blender for food preparation. In

her mother's time they had not had those comforts; her mother used the grating slab for preparing the seasonings and grinding the spices. Mona ate well and slept well, and her family lived in their own house. It would be unfair to say that her life was a complete misery.

Akbar Ahmad suddenly looked pleased, as if she had finally got the point he had been trying to make all that time.

She began feeling irritated with Hina for talking about Akbar Ahmad before her in that manner. She blamed herself, too, for not saying a single word in Akbar Ahmad's defence. She had allowed herself to be swayed by Hina's opinions. She felt that Akbar Ahmad had sensed that she secretly endorsed Hina's views. That was the reason he looked hurt. A man needs peace in his grave, she thought as she took a last sip of her tea.

Nobody's good enough for Hina, Akbar Ahmad had often said, and he spoke the truth. Hadn't Hina said all manner of things about Salamat Ali, too, today?

Suddenly Mona felt guilty for thinking of Salamat Ali in Akbar Ahmad's presence.

She thought about visiting the graveyard that weekend to say a prayer for Akbar Ahmad's soul. On the anniversary of his death she had gone with Tanya and Amber. She had to do her own little penance for allowing Akbar Ahmad to be rebuked in her presence and for thinking of Salamat Ali in his.

Mona could not go to visit Akbar Ahmad's grave because Hina invited her to spend a week at her house. *You need some time away from Salamat Ali and Mrs. Baig,* Hina had told her. *Just to clear your mind. It would be good for you.*

Mona was grateful to get away from the scene of her recent emotional turmoil.

The preparations did not take long. Mrs. Baig offered to keep an eye on the house, so Mona left an extra key with her. Mrs. Baig did not bring up the subject of Salamat Ali's letter, although Mona thought she looked inquiringly at her as she said goodbye. When she returned home, Mona gave some last-minute instructions to Noori and Habib and brought her bag into the living room to wait for Hina. Suddenly, she caught sight of Akbar Ahmad's portrait.

After Akbar Ahmad's death, she had sometimes stayed overnight at Hina's house. She often felt curiously restless and realized that unconsciously perhaps she could not bring herself to leave Akbar Ahmad alone in the house; it was as if she felt a need to attend to him. Now he would be by himself for a whole week. He had a needy look on his face.

Did Akbar Ahmad know what was going on in her mind? she wondered. But he seemed more concerned about his loneliness than about Mona's thoughts. She realized that at one level their relationship had remained unchanged. As long as Akbar Ahmad's needs were addressed, her purpose in *his* life was fully served. He made no effort to know what she was thinking. It was perhaps best that her thoughts remained hidden from him, Mona told herself.

When she heard Hina's car horn in the street, she got her bag and left.

THE WEEK-LONG VISIT at Hina's house had an unintended effect on Mona.

She had never stayed there for an extended period of time, so she had not had a chance to witness the domestic details of her sister's life. But now she analyzed the daily interactions between Jafar and Hina. Jafar not only deferred to Hina's decisions in household matters, but also discussed his business matters with her, frequently asking her advice.

Seeing how Jafar conducted himself towards Hina, Mona understood why Hina exuded the confidence she herself lacked as a woman. She remembered that when she was young, she had been more outgoing than Hina. The feeling that she had missed out on the pleasures of married life grew inside her. She realized she felt envious of Hina.

Perhaps self-respect had kept Mona from making a comparison between Akbar Ahmad and Jafar, but she could not help making a comparison between Akbar Ahmad and Salamat Ali, the first man who had shown her attention and seemed to care about her.

WHEN JAFAR DROPPED Mona at home after her visit, she invited him in for tea. While she was chatting with her brother-in-law, Amber phoned to say that her daughter was sick. Would Mona come spend the weekend with her? Mona's things were already in the car, as Jafar had not brought them in yet. He offered to drop Mona at Amber's house.

When Mona arrived at Amber's house, she asked Jafar to tell Hina about the change in plans. They had decided to go shopping after the weekend.

~~~

ON MONDAY HINA called at Amber's house and took Mona shopping with her. In one of the smaller stalls at the Zainab Market, Mona saw a pair of silver filigree earrings that she liked, and tried them on. They suited her. Hina insisted on buying them for her.

"This is my gift for you. I did not bring anything for you from Islamabad when I was there."

"You didn't have to. It's not as if you went out of the country," Mona said.

When Hina thrust the money into the vendor's hand before Mona could even open her purse, she finally relented, and allowed her sister to lead her away.

Later, Mona helped Hina choose a few bedsheets and tablecloths. They had a late lunch at a Chinese restaurant. Mona had chosen it because she liked its continental dessert menu. Hina insisted on also paying the lunch bill. After the dessert, Mona felt drowsy. Hina said she would take her home.

When they were stopped at a traffic light, Hina said, "I finally met your Salamat Ali today."

"Where? When?" Mona was surprised. "You're telling me now?"

"I'd been meaning to ask you to arrange a meeting for some time," Hina said, looking at the road. "I didn't know you were visiting Amber. When I went to your place today and didn't find you there, I looked in at Mrs. Baig's to check if you were with her. And there was Salamat Ali, with Mrs. Baig gushing over him. Anyway, it was about time we met and talked. Don't you think?" Hina turned and glanced at Mona.

"Well, now that you have met him . . . ?" Mona asked.

"He was very nice to me," Hina answered. "And he likes you very much, I could tell. That alone should be enough to convince me."

"And yet?" Mona said after a brief silence.

"I still object to his appearance—not that it's something that can't be fixed. The main thing was that he answered a little evasively about his business."

"Maybe he didn't wish to talk in front of Mrs. Baig."

"Maybe."

Later Mona wondered if Hina was being truthful in saying that Jafar had forgotten to tell her about Mona's plan to visit Amber. She clearly remembered asking him to do so. She wondered why Hina had conducted that surprise interview with Salamat Ali, and felt irked with her sister again.

MONA'S FRUSTRATION GREW as she went indoors. She began critically judging Hina's relationship with Jafar. Was it as perfect as it seemed? If it was, why did her sister spend so much time prying into Mona's affairs? She was exhausted from all this emotional stress. In such a state of mind she did not wish to have to contend with Akbar Ahmad's silent remonstrations too, so she stayed well away from the living room where she knew he would be waiting for her.

Later, she had to get some water, and the living room offered the shortest way into the kitchen. She avoided looking at the portrait on the way in, but coming out, as she turned to close the door behind her, she saw him.

Mona's ears rang with what Akbar Ahmad had told her many years ago. *If you think that Hina is against me, you are wrong. What she's really against is your happiness.* As she looked at his eyes, she sensed a rare empathy in them. She tried unsuccessfully to recall the occasion when he had said that about Hina. Was Akbar Ahmad right, after all? Now his expression was smug.

Standing there, Mona finally remembered when Akbar Ahmad had made those remarks about her sister. She had returned tearful from a visit to Hina's house during which Hina had tried to convince Mona to leave her husband. She had already spoken to Jafar and he was willing to support Mona and her daughters. Mona had refused. Akbar Ahmad had had no way of knowing what Hina had told her. He could only guess, judging from the caustic remarks Hina let slip about him every time they met. Mona wondered now if he had known more than he let on.

Akbar Ahmad apparently had a sixth sense in certain matters. The few times that they went shopping together, he seemed to know when Mona really liked something. He would pre-empt her by remarking on the need to better organize the household budget and shun extravagance in daily life. Mona asked herself why, if Akbar Ahmad had guessed the content of her discussions with Hina, there had been no change in his behaviour towards her. It was hard to explain, unless Akbar Ahmad really cared so little about her that he would choose his own comfort over ending her unhappiness. Mona could not bring herself to accept this, but the thought made her angry all the same. Thinking of Akbar Ahmad and Hina's motives, Mona realized that at least her sister's actions could never be prompted by ill-feeling or malice towards her.

MONA HAD SKIPPED several days of her outdoor walks while she was away at Amber's. Today she was enjoying being out with Mrs. Baig. Recent surprise rains had washed the trees and they looked greener. The leaves shone in the light of the setting sun.

"I am planning something for you, Mona," Mrs. Baig said as they entered the park.

"Aren't you done planning for me yet?" Mona laughed, as she walked around a small puddle of water in the pathway. "What is it this time?"

"It's a surprise!" Mrs. Baig said.

Mona wondered what it was, but knew there was no use pushing Mrs. Baig to tell her.

A few days after that conversation, Hina called Mona to invite her for tea at her house.

"Any particular occasion?" Mona asked.

"Is an occasion needed to have a cup of tea?"

"If you have invited Tanya and Amber, I will get a ride with one of them."

"No, the girls won't be there. Jafar will pick you up at six p.m. from your place."

Mona wondered if this was the surprise Mrs. Baig had been talking about. Now she saw Hina's visit to Mrs. Baig's house in a new light. She could imagine a conspiracy between Hina and Mrs. Baig. Once before, Hina had sought Mrs. Baig's help to find out what Mona wanted for

her birthday. It was entirely likely that Mrs. Baig had discreetly arranged to introduce Salamat Ali to the family on
this occasion.

Mona decided to sound out Amber and Tanya. They both
told her that they were busy that evening. Mona decided
not to ask about the nature of their engagements. She
became convinced that they, too, were in on the secret.

Jafar picked up Mona from her house on the appointed
day. Mona had dressed up for the occasion, while trying not
to draw too much attention to the fact. She had specially
worn the silver earrings Hina had bought her.

As they entered through the gate and were passing by
the tall hedge that enclosed the garden, Mona heard Hina's
laughter. She heard a man's voice, too. She immediately
recognized it as that of Jafar's cousin, Imad.

She turned. "Is Imad here?" she asked Jafar.

Jafar looked at her. "Well, I was not supposed to let you
in on the surprise but I guess Hina has just blown it herself.
Yes, Imad is here. Hina thought—We both thought that perhaps the two of you should meet. Now that he's in Karachi—"

"I guess Tanya and Amber are not invited?"

"No. No. I thought Hina had told you. We did not want a
big crowd, you know—"

"Can I just have a moment by myself, Jafar?" Mona
interrupted him.

"Of course! Of course!" Jafar said. "You know where the
washrooms are. Hina has also left the bedroom door open
in case you need anything from her dresser."

Mona stood there for a few moments waiting for Jafar to
go into the garden and join Hina. She was feeling humili-

ated. Ordinarily, she would not have had any objection to meeting Imad socially at Hina's house, but she felt that Hina had once more proved officious by forcing Imad's company on her in this manner. As if conducting surprise interviews with Salamat Ali without her knowledge were not enough!

Let them enjoy their high-tea together, Mona said to herself. Without telling anyone, she angrily left Hina's house. She kept walking until she found a taxi to take her home.

Mona's house was a half hour drive from Hina's but the taxi driver took her on a longer route saying that one of the roads on the shorter route were blocked. By the time Mona reached home it had been over an hour since she left Hina's house.

SHORTLY AFTER MONA'S return home, she heard a car outside. She looked out her window to see Hina at the gate, a worried look on her face.

"Why are you all doing this to me?" Mona said as she brought Hina inside, her voice trembling and tears in her eyes.

"I am sorry, Mona," Hina said gently. "I did not mean to hurt you."

Mona remained quiet.

"Why did you leave like that?" her sister asked.

Mona laughed mockingly. She sensed the guilt in Hina's voice, but it did not appease her. "Because you seemed to have made up your mind about what is good for me."

"Please don't take to heart anything I said before," Hina said. "I was not sure how you would ultimately decide. Now that I know—"

Mona realized that Hina had articulated her decision for her. Even with the entire chain of preceding events it had not seemed inevitable to her that she would come to it in the end.

"Shhh." Hina hugged her as Mona began sobbing. "Don't cry now. I am sorry. I told you I am sorry. Jafar also felt bad when you left suddenly like that. He blamed me for forcing you into meeting Imad. I am sorry. I realize my mistake."

Mona finally stopped crying.

"I'm sure your Salamat Ali is a better man," Hina said, caressing Mona's hair, "if his letter to you is anything to go by. I'm certain Akbar Ahmad could never have written that letter. Especially the last part. A letter from him would have been full of conditions and hidden threats. And the story of the flowers and the cinema ticket. What a jolly seducer. If I sounded harsh it was because I didn't want you to have to undergo another—" Hina stopped.

Mona was looking at her with tears in her eyes.

The two sisters stood together for a while. Then Hina led Mona by her arm to the chairs in the garden.

Neither of them said anything for some time.

"Your garden looks really lovely now." Hina was looking around. "But then, you always loved gardens. Remember when you were small, how your clothes always smelled of fresh grass from rolling on the lawn? You spent so much time there that you even learned to mimic the sound of all the birds that nested in our garden."

Mona did remember. She even had a reputation as a tomboy. She was the only girl in the family who could whistle and who played with the boys.

Mona recalled the competitions for spinning tops from which she had been excluded because it was considered a boys-only domain. She secretly practised spinning at home and perfected the difficult and dangerous technique of throwing and catching the spinning top on the flat of her palm. Hina, too, had been tempted to try it, but gave up in fright when she saw a top graze Mona's temple, narrowly missing her eye. Once the boys saw Mona's expertise with the top they never again excluded her from their games.

During their mother's illness, she had undergone a slow change, becoming more reserved and emotional, witnessing her mother's long struggle with cancer, the hope of her recovery proffered by the doctors, and then the sudden relapses—one of which ultimately claimed her life. Mona had had her first struggle with depression when their father died within a few years of their mother's death. After that, Hina had taken over the role of both parents for Mona.

Hina interrupted her thoughts. "I forgot to ask you. Has anyone checked Salamat Ali's references yet to verify his history?"

"Mrs. Baig told me she had," Mona replied.

"She's silly. I can't rely on her judgment. I'll get Jafar to check them. I'll call you to get the information when I get home." She paused.

"Another thing: It's not that you'd be financially dependent on him—the estate now belongs to you and the girls. Still, if you don't mind, I'll ask Jafar to arrange with our lawyer to secure your assets beforehand. It's always better to be safe in these matters."

Mona was silent.

"Do something else for me," she said after a moment.

"The girls?" Hina asked.

Mona nodded.

Hina sounded thoughtful. "As you haven't told them of your decision yet, let me break the news to them. They might find it less upsetting, hearing it from me."

"Tanya will be very unhappy. She couldn't even accept—"

"What about Amber?"

"I don't know how she'll react. I did not discuss the matter with her at all while I was at her place. At least she hadn't confronted me like Tanya did, although she was the one who received Aunt Aneesa's call!"

"Poor Amber. She's so sweet. Tanya—well! But don't worry about the girls, as I said. Leave them to me. I just can't wait to see the expression on Mrs. Kazi's face when *she* gets the news."

They both laughed, imagining Mrs. Kazi's horror.

Mona walked Hina to her car. "What do you think Jafar will say?" she asked, just before Hina drove away. "Will he be upset?"

"Don't worry about him. Leave him to me. If he has any problems, I'll also go and find another man! Remember, I'm just two years older than you!"

All the anxiety and depression that Mona had felt in recent days was gone. She felt exhausted, but happy.

"Come, don't start crying again now," Hina said.

V

ADAPTATION

Three days later, Mona dialled Hina's number several times in the afternoon but without success. Mona wished to talk with Hina to find out Amber's thoughts. Hina had told her she would be speaking to her that morning. Mona felt restless and was irritated by the continuous busy signal on Hina's phone. She sent Habib to flag down a taxi for her to go to Hina's house.

Mona found Hina sitting on her porch under the awning, reading a magazine.

"I called your house a little earlier and Habib told me that you had already left," Hina said, as Mona climbed the wooden steps of the porch.

"Your phone was busy the whole afternoon," Mona said.

"I was talking with Amber. Then Jafar phoned to ask me to read him one of the letters he had received."

"What did Amber say?"

"I'll tell you. Let's go inside."

As they entered the living room, they heard a car in the driveway.

"That must be Jafar." Hina said. "He must have finished his meetings early today."

"You were telling me about Amber."

"She has more or less accepted the situation."

"What did she say?"

"I really didn't expect her to put up a fight or anything like that. I was more interested in finding out what she could tell me about Tanya's thoughts."

"Did you find out anything?"

"No, I didn't, and that's promising."

"What do you mean?"

"I mean that if there was some sort of agreement between the girls, I would have received an impression of it, or she would have given me some hint. She could have left the tough talk to Tanya."

"That doesn't mean she has accepted it herself."

"You cannot have everyone else's happiness in mind as well when you go out seeking your own. It's not as if what you wish to do with your life is going to take away anything from theirs. For you that should be enough," Hina said, sitting down. "Don't expect the whole world to gather around and offer you its blessings for every choice you make in your life. It doesn't work like that."

They were interrupted by voices in the corridor. Both Hina and Mona were taken aback to see Mrs. Kazi enter the room, followed by Tanya.

"Yes, I know. You can take your time and finish whatever

you came to do here. I will talk to Hina or Jafar," Mrs. Kazi was saying. "It is not as if I insist on going everywhere with you every day. But once in a while I also feel like an outing. You never have any time for me. Hina, so nice to see you. Oh! Mona is also here. I was just telling Tanya that she should not cut me off so completely from her family. I have nobody to talk to all day."

"You are welcome to visit any time you wish," Mona said, as Tanya passed her by in a huff and sat down at the other end of the sofa.

Hina got up to arrange the cushions on the sofa and make room for Mrs. Kazi.

After the tea was served, Mrs. Kazi stirred the artificial sweetener into her cup, took a sip, made a face, and stared hard at Mona, who avoided her gaze by looking away.

"If I knew you were coming," Hina addressed Tanya, "I would have asked the cook to make some snacks before he left."

Tanya ignored Hina's comment and said, "I spoke to Amber and she told me you had called."

Hina was silent for a few moments. Mona noticed that Mrs. Kazi sat up straighter.

"I meant to call you in the evening when you returned from work," Hina said.

"I didn't go to work today," Tanya grumbled.

Mrs. Kazi looked at Mona. "Please do tell me what this is all about. I am, after all, family. There's no relation as close as the mother-in-law of your daughter."

"It's nothing," Tanya said brusquely.

Mrs. Kazi ignored Tanya's comment and smiled knowingly. "I do not wish to intrude, Mona. I heard a few things about all that's going on with your plans to remarry."

"It is still too early to say anything," Hina said quickly.

Mona felt relieved at her intervention.

"Too early?" Mrs. Kazi said incredulously. "I heard otherwise. In any case, you have been such a good wife and mother, Mona, that I was surprised to hear that. Very surprised."

Mona felt trapped. Tanya was staring angrily at a point above her head. Mona opened her mouth to say something, but Hina gestured to her to remain silent.

Mrs. Kazi now addressed Hina. "You must discourage her, Hina, from throwing away the labour of a lifetime. A woman's reputation is all that she gains in this life. And this talk of a proposal of marriage—isn't it also a little too late in the day?"

"My mother lost her husband when she was much younger," Mrs. Kazi continued, without noticing Hina's hardening expression. "Yet no man saw even a glimpse of her small finger till the day she died."

"First of all, Mrs. Kazi, " Hina said, "our religion doesn't forbid a widow from marrying. Secondly, Mona isn't as old as you think. When she goes out with Amber, people often mistake the two of them for sisters."

"How old are you then, Mona?" Mrs. Kazi asked, then added, "But I was only saying that—"

"Yes, please tell me what you were saying," Hina retorted before Mona could reply. "That our religion allows a widow to marry again but you don't agree with that? That you're a greater authority than God and His Prophet?"

"Since when did *you* start quoting religious law, Hina?" Mrs. Kazi shot back. "In all these years I've seen you say your prayers only during Ramazan."

"That's right. I don't care for false piety, just as I have no pretensions to religious knowledge, but I can at least tell you what every child knows about religion. I also brought it up, Mrs. Kazi, because you were carrying on about your mother's little finger."

Mona could not hide her smile. She felt strangely calm now.

"What is objectionable must be voiced!" Mrs. Kazi replied haughtily.

"And who made you, by the way, the authority to pronounce something objectionable?" Hina asked. "While we're on the subject, the one thing that I do find objectionable is your gossiping about my sister to your relatives."

Mrs. Kazi cast Tanya a dark look. Mona enjoyed her discomfort.

"Gossiping, in case you need a reminder," Hina said, "is something expressly forbidden by our religion. If you have even half the fear of God you pretend, you'd do penance for your actions as soon as you get home."

"I haven't said anything to anyone of which I should be ashamed," Mrs. Kazi said to Hina. "*You* should be ashamed, in fact, for treating your guests in this manner."

"I'm sorry," Hina said icily. "You're your own guest here today because you came uninvited."

For a moment Mrs. Kazi sat shocked into silence. Mona felt that Hina had gone too far. Mrs. Kazi banged her teacup onto the tea trolley and rose.

"Come, Tanya!" she said. "I'm leaving. I can't take this any more. I've never been so gravely insulted in all my life!"

Mona finally spoke. "Please sit down, Mrs. Kazi—"

Tanya looked first at Mrs. Kazi, who was moving towards the door, then at Hina.

"Driver!" Mrs. Kazi called out from the door. "Tanya! Come with me!"

Hina made a gesture to Tanya.

Tanya spoke up. "You can take the car, Mrs, Kazi. I'll have Aunt Hina drop me home later."

"Go with her, Tanya," Mona said. She felt anxious and worried, but Tanya would not look at her and ignored what she said.

Mrs. Kazi apparently wanted to say something to Tanya in reply, but Hina got up and stood between them. Mrs. Kazi did not dare speak.

Jafar walked in a moment later. Mona was arguing with Hina. Tanya was sitting on the sofa, smiling indifferently.

"Hello, Mona. How are you, Tanya? What's going on?" he asked. "I just saw Mrs. Kazi leave. She looked unhappy. Didn't even reply when I said hello."

"Aunt Hina can be so mean sometimes." Tanya laughed.

"No matter what we think of Mrs. Kazi, we can't address her like that, Hina," said Mona, as Hina sat down next to Tanya. "We have married Tanya into her family."

"That's the only way you can silence people like her,"

Hina said, and turned towards Tanya. "Tell me, now, what time does Faraz get off from work?"

"In about forty-five minutes. Why?" Tanya asked.

"Maybe you can tell me, Hina, what happened here," Jafar asked, half smiling, half serious.

"I will tell you all, but first do me a favour and drop Tanya at Faraz's office," Hina said.

"But you asked me to stay," Tanya protested.

"Only so that Mrs. Kazi does not pester you on the way home."

"Can't Uncle Jafar drop Mummy home instead," Tanya whispered as she leaned conspiratorially towards Hina. "Then we can talk."

"Later. You must go straight to Faraz's office now and take him out for dinner or shopping or something else. Let Mrs. Kazi stew in her own bile for a few hours. You don't want her to have Faraz's ear after what happened here."

"The suspense is killing me," Jafar said. "Would some-one tell me please what's going on?"

Hina ignored him. "Go now, Tanya. There's no time to lose. You should catch Faraz before he leaves. In fact, give him a call from here and let him know you're on your way so that he waits for you."

While Tanya made the call to Faraz, Jafar asked no more questions.

"I thought we had agreed, Hina, that we will handle Tanya with care," Mona said as soon as Jafar and Tanya left. "Faraz might take offence at your treatment of his mother. You have compromised Tanya's position."

"Don't worry," Hina said with a dismissive wave of her hand. "Nothing will happen with Faraz. He's a wimp. We both know that Tanya married him for that very reason. Once Mrs. Kazi started it, I had to make sure she wouldn't have the gall to speak ill of you in front of Tanya again. I'm very grateful that Mrs. Kazi invited herself here today. It was wonderful to have you here as well. We couldn't have asked for a better opportunity."

"But still, you insulted her in my presence."

"You have nothing to worry about. My house is neutral grounds. The bitch had come to pour out her venom against you and was looking for a chance to do it in front of Tanya. Do you think I should have offered her garlands?"

HINA AND MONA were in the kitchen having another round of tea when Jafar returned.

He laughed after Hina finished telling him about Mrs. Kazi's visit. "May God save me from women and their devices!"

"Really?" Hina arched her brow. "Now, why on earth would you want that?"

"Um, maybe no."

Hina handed him a teacup. "I am sure you know what is good for you."

"I am sure," Jafar said, winking at Mona affectedly, and stirring his tea. "So, what's the plan now?"

"Same as before. We were just discussing what we must tell all other relatives. They don't have to be slain like Mrs. Kazi and Aunt Aneesa. They just need a mouthful of an explanation to recite when other people ask them about the depravity and scandal that's about to engulf our pious family."

"There're some standard things that everyone finds acceptable." Jafar put down the teacup and crossed his arms. "That it's just a marriage of convenience because Mona needed someone who could manage the estate she had come into after Akbar Ahmad's death. Tanya and Amber can say that it was the family elders who decided their mother needed someone to care for her in her old age. Remember to emphasize old age and disease."

"Old age and disease, my God!" Hina said with mock exasperation. "Do you realize that we're older than Mona and Salamat Ali?"

"We are the family elders now." Jafar raised a finger. "Old age and disease come with the territory. Also, don't forget to mention that in general it's good to have a man around the house—for running errands, attending on the woman of the house and, most importantly, guarding her honour, as yours truly has done for many years."

"You are becoming smart little by little, I can see that." Hina smiled as she looked into Jafar's eyes. "How do you do that?"

"By keeping smart company, of course," Jafar said, picking up his tea.

"Of course," Hina replied.

Mona laughed, feeling a sense of relief. The reassurance that she could draw on Hina's support and her clear-headed advice in the matter helped Mona rediscover the sense of self-possession that had long eluded her. She felt bad for doubting Hina's motives. They were only guided by a concern for her well-being, she told herself. Mona realized that if she were to change places with Hina, she would perhaps act similarly. The only thing that mattered was that Hina had stood by her side. Her sister had been there for her all these years, too, but her support now gave Mona a feeling that she would be able to cope with anything.

After speaking to Tanya, Hina called on Mona and reassured her that she should not fear a common front from her daughters. They did seem to have reservations but no such strong objections that might bring them together to oppose Mona in her decision.

TWO DAYS LATER, when Mona sat down to write the reply to Salamat Ali's letter, she suddenly realized that it was not simply a matter of expressing her consent. Her situation demanded that the reply reflect the concerns of someone in her situation. She must represent the image of a mother, as well as that of a respectable widow. This latter image repulsed her because it traditionally represented someone who deserved society's pity. She did not need anyone's pity, and, moreover, the proposal was initiated by Salamat Ali, not by her or her family. She may be a widow but she was completely independent, financially as well as in other respects. She would have to state this forcefully without offending Salamat Ali. Then there was the matter of the residence. She did not know what plans Salamat Ali had for it but she could not imagine moving out of her house. She would have to explain that, too. The idea of living in his wife's house might offend his ego, but there was no helping it. Knowing Salamat Ali, she would also have to couch her consent of his proposal in such terms that he did not take it as a signal to take further liberties with her. She realized her reply was beginning to look more and more like a business transaction, but in her situation it could only be that—not a love letter. She had never written one in her life, but she imagined that if she had, she would not have had to be so careful in expressing herself. The thought saddened her that even the mere promise of the happiness that had eluded her so far should be embraced with such caution.

She felt too overwhelmed to think any more about it, and put the pen and paper away.

The next day when she sat down to write, another emotion impeded her. She felt afraid. Had she gone too far in trying to make a point to Sajid Mir and Aunt Aneesa? Was she overreacting to her daughters' natural concern for her well-being, and her sister's abiding interest in securing a better future for her? Wasn't it a path she had dismissed not too long ago as unbecoming for someone in her circumstances? And how prepared was she to start a new life with someone about whom she knew very little? What if everything turned out worse than before? And was it reasonable for a mother of two grown-up daughters to seek marital fulfillment? These thoughts kept recurring, as did the fear of the potential consequences of her decision. She thought she should take some more time before she made her response.

But by morning the feeling had passed, and she finally finished writing the letter. After putting away the pen, as she leaned back to relax, her eyes met Akbar Ahmad's anxious gaze. For the last few days she had not felt his presence. Now Mona sat up, took the pen from the drawer and rewrote the letter, adding to its contents. She reread it and was satisfied with its tone and substance. She thought that Akbar Ahmad also seemed more at ease.

A FEW DAYS LATER, Mona noticed that Noori, Habib, and the gardener were avoiding eye contact, and occasionally she caught them looking at her a little strangely. Noori finally approached her and asked, "Mona bibi, are you going to marry Mrs. Baig's tenant?"

"Who told you?" Mona asked.

From Noori's long and confusing account, Mona gathered that the rumours had originated with Aunt Aneesa and were carried to Tanya's house by the washerwoman who did the laundry in both houses. She had confided in Tanya's driver, who spread the gossip further when he came to Mona's house early that morning to return some crockery Tanya had borrowed from Mona for a party.

Once the apparent facts were known, Habib and the gardener took great offence to Salamat Ali's blatant assault on the dignity of their employer, the respectable widow Mrs. Akbar Ahmad. Only Noori seemed excited by the prospect.

"CAN I READ IT?" Mrs. Baig pleaded, when Mona gave her the letter for Salamat Ali.

Mona laughed. "Of course you can read it."

Earlier, when Mona had phoned Mrs. Baig to tell her that she had a letter she would like her to give to Salamat Ali, Mrs. Baig said, "Wait!" The next moment Mona saw her come almost sprinting from her gate to the kitchen door.

Mrs. Baig read the letter carefully, without sitting down. Then she embraced Mona and without a word hurried away, the letter hidden under the folds of her sari, in the same manner she had brought her Salamat Ali's letter some weeks ago.

Mr. Salamat Ali,

I received your letter some time ago through Mrs. Baig, an old family friend and someone I trust and respect.

I thank you for the consideration you showed in asking my opinion before approaching anyone else in my family with your proposal. It so happened that Mrs. Baig, in her anxiety, informed some members of my family at the same time that she delivered your letter, and I ran into opposition from them even before I had a chance to consider your proposal. It all happened for the best, perhaps, because I was forced to regard your proposal with full realization of the consequences it holds for me and my immediate family. Such hasty reactions are understandable in these circumstances and they do not reflect any judgment of you as a person—those who raised the objections had not met you.

I cannot accept your proposal without clarification of certain doubts and concerns that I have regarding it, some of which I have already expressed. Our continued meetings without establishing a respectable relationship will give rise to unnecessary gossip and slander that will not only affect my honour and reputation—and the well-being and happiness of my daughters and their families—but also cast you in an unfavourable light. The first possibility is unacceptable to me and the second would be unfair to you. The present situation requires a solution that circumvents these consequences. /

Once you have clarified your position and we have decided to follow through with the matter of your proposal, there will be other matters which will await solution.

You have accepted me as I am without conditions and I will make very few conditions on my part. I am used to my house and do not feel a desire to change my residence. I wish to continue living in my home and I hope you will not object to it. Likewise, I would like to maintain my financial independence in all matters.

As you know, too, I have two daughters who are both married with families. I would need to make sure that they do not feel any change in my feelings towards them, or in my relationship to them as their mother. I should continue to have time for them as before and, under the changed circumstances, may have to do so even a little more conscientiously. Nor would I ever wish to make them feel that the change in my status has in any way desecrated the memory of their deceased father, Mr. Akbar Ahmad, who loved them dearly and who was very dear to me, too. We have always cherished the memory of him as a loving father and husband and will continue to do so for the rest of our lives. Which leads me to my final stipulation: In honour of his memory, we keep a portrait of Mr. Akbar Ahmad in the house. You will find it hanging in the living room, where it will remain as long as I call this place my home.

In all other matters I hope we will endeavour to make our decisions with due regard for each other's feelings and wishes.

While we carefully consider these matters and our circumstances, I request you to be careful about how we present ourselves in front of our family. In view of the existing objections from some members of the family, they must not be given any chance to speak against the propriety of our conduct. I would be immensely distressed if such a thing were to happen. I have to mention this in no uncertain terms because, on account of your forced attentions in the recent past, I have no choice but to discourage you from taking further liberties in the strongest possible terms.

While we maintain an unimpeachable relationship, the tensions and distrust about your proposal will disappear soon enough, and if we do take the final step in the end, everyone will put aside their presumptions and prejudices to accept you as another member of the family. That is all I can hope for. There's nothing that I can do to make your entry into the family any easier. If you wish to pursue this suit you must accept these conditions, because when you sent me your proposal my status was not hidden from you, and since you are part of the same society, I am sure you expected some opposition of this nature. Even if you did not, it should not come as a complete surprise to you. I hope that you will have the good judgment to accept it as the justifiable reaction from those who have nothing but my best interests at heart.

I shall await your reply to all the issues I have raised in this letter.

Sincerely,

Mrs. Mona Akbar Ahmad

~~~

SALAMAT ALI'S ANSWER came swiftly. The handwriting slanted even more sharply towards the edge.

My dearest Mona,

I cannot tell you how honoured I feel by your reply. To become the companion of someone as beautiful as you is beyond my wildest dreams! As I mentioned before, it was some misunderstandings that caused your displeasure. I apologize unconditionally. I would like nothing more than to see you happy and I will undertake any labour to prove to you that I mean it. Will you forgive me now? Tell me you will, otherwise life will become too burdensome for me.

I do not fear people's prejudgments and I do not take offence at people's prejudices. I look forward to an opportunity to meet your relatives to set their minds at ease about me. I salute you for bravely facing their objections and thinking with an independent mind. I fully agree with you that we must get married as soon as possible. It will show everyone that my intentions are noble and my character without blemish. I will then begin the greater task of proving my love and sincerity to you.

Although I would have wished to start our lives anew in all respects, I would not even dream of displacing you against your wishes and therefore I must accept your kind invitation to live in your house. I do not have too many belongings as I have a frugal lifestyle and whatever little there is can easily fit into a corner of a room if you would kindly allow me to have one. And I will always respect your financial independence.

I recently had the pleasure of meeting your daughters and I immediately felt a filial affection towards them. While I cannot take the place of their real father, they can always rely on me to act as their father in all respects. Of course you must devote all the time you wish to your daughters. Since I already look upon them as my own daughters, I insist that you carry out all your duties to them as their mother before you perform any to me as my wife. I can also assure you that I will never object to the presence of Mr. Akbar Ahmad's portrait in the house. Any object worthy of veneration for you is for me equally so, if not more so.

I also swear by you that in all matters big and small I will never take a step without your happy consent. In

*fact, I hereby give the control of my life fully into your
hands. You make the decisions and I will comply. I will
not be happy with anything less. I would very much like
us to go to a movie sometime soon. Or we can go for a
picnic. I make very tasty kebab rolls. I am sure you will
like them. I hope you will not refuse this invitation.*

Yours forever,

Salamat

~~~

Mr. Salamat Ali,

*I take your word as the word of an honest and truthful
man and accept your explanations and clarifications.
I am happy that you understand my circumstances. I am
grateful to you, as well, for accepting the few things I asked
of you. As I had mentioned, I expect us to maintain an
honourable comportment within the view of my family
and society. We must not see each other alone until our
relationship is formalized. Similarly, I also request you to
continue addressing me as Mrs. Mona Akbar Ahmad
until such time. You may, if you wish, communicate
through correspondence.*

Sincerely,

Mrs. Mona Akbar Ahmad

~~~

Dear Mrs. Mona Akbar Ahmad,

*Please forgive my indiscretion. I hope you will
forgive someone who forgot himself for an instant in his*

ecstasy. I look with happy anticipation at the time
when I can address you with terms of endearment.
In the meanwhile I am happy to do any penance you
suggest. I shall wait for your response.

   Very sincerely yours,
   Salamat Ali

~~~

Mr. Salamat Ali,

   Thank you for your note. No penance is required
by me, nor is it necessary. My sister Hina and her
husband, Jafar, have invited you for dinner at their
house on Friday night. The address is enclosed. There
you will also formally meet my daughters and their
families. Some other relatives are also invited. You will
find all of them welcoming. My sister has arranged
for Mrs. Baig to be picked up at seven p.m. that evening
and mentioned that if you so wish, and find it conven-
ient, you may accompany her.

   Sincerely,
   Mrs. Mona Akbar Ahmad

MONA SENT HER LAST LETTER on a Monday. The next day Mrs. Baig told her that she would like to invite Mona and Salamat Ali to a restaurant for dinner before the family gathering at Hina's house. "I had been planning to do it for some time now—as I told you that day in the park—but I was busy last week with the women's club meeting. There will be no harm done," Mrs. Baig added when she saw the hesitant look on Mona's face. "You've no reason to fear any member of your family seeing you, since I will be there with you. If I had not made that absolutely clear to Salamat Ali, I wouldn't have agreed to the idea."

"The idea was his?"

"Yes, yes, he was insistent, and I saw no harm in the two of you getting to know each other a little better before meeting other members of your family. But I told him I'll pay for the dinner, as a gift to both of you. If you still feel uneasy, I'll invite Hina too."

"No, that's okay," Mona said quickly, "I'll have no concerns if you're there."

She was thinking that Mrs. Baig's presence could easily be disregarded, but in Hina's presence, Salamat Ali might feel a little self-conscious. She herself might feel uncomfortable under the gaze of both Mrs. Baig and her sister.

"And I don't want to add to the bill," Mona declared to make sure Mrs. Baig saw the wisdom of not including Hina. "That would be unfair. You're already doing so much for me."

"I hadn't thought of that, you know," Mrs. Baig said, before realizing that she had been thinking aloud. "I don't worry about the expense. No, I'm not worried about the expense. It's only because you're telling me that it's okay with you—"

BEFORE GOING UPSTAIRS to their table in the restaurant, Mrs. Baig left a message for Salamat Ali with the hostess at the reception. The note said that he would find them in the dining area. As they climbed the stairs, Mrs. Baig commented on the increasing number of girls being hired by hotel chains at hospitality desks. "That's one good change," she said. "At least the girls listen to what someone is saying."

After they were seated, Mona glanced down over the railing and saw Salamat Ali walking towards the reception. She could not tell whether he had just arrived or had been in the lobby when they came in.

"Yes, Mrs. Baig, but the girls should also behave more professionally. They shouldn't give the impression that they're flirting when talking to male customers." Mona felt a rising consternation as the hostess who was talking to Salamat Ali played with her hair and smiled.

Soon Salamat Ali was on his way up.

Salamat Ali was about to sit next to Mona, but Mrs. Baig pointed to the seat next to hers. Mona wished Mrs. Baig were a little less officious in her duties as chaperone. Salamat Ali ended up sitting opposite Mona at the table for four. As Mona looked at Mrs. Baig sitting between them, she could sense how Mrs. Baig's daughter-in-law must have felt while staying in her house. Mona was thankful, however, for Mrs. Baig's taking charge of the conversation.

"I feel responsible for both of you. Your whole future relationship is a test of my judgment," Mrs. Baig said.

"We will never let you down, Mrs. Baig!" Salamat Ali said, looking at Mona.

Mona had to smile out of politeness.

"To tell you the truth, I feel a greater duty towards Mona," Mrs. Baig said. "She's shown implicit faith in my judgment by accepting this proposal."

"I'm sure Mona, er, I mean Mrs. Akbar Ahmad will never have reason—"

"You can call her Mona now. It's only a matter of weeks now before you will anyway, you know," Mrs. Baig said with a patronizing smile.

Mona threw a quick glance in Mrs. Baig's direction but said nothing.

Salamat Ali seemed to feel emboldened. "Yes, I mean Mona will forever feel grateful to you for your suggestion."

Mrs. Baig wagged a finger at him in gentle admonition, then added, "And I feel confident that you'll be as caring towards Mona as you proved helpful and industrious around my house." Mrs. Baig's sense of justice was stirred as Salamat Ali's appreciative landlady.

"Don't say that! You're embarrassing me," Salamat Ali protested.

His feet beat a tattoo on the floor and several times Mona felt his leg brush against hers under the table.

"What did I ever do for you, other than help you with small tasks around the house? A little bit of this and a little bit of that. I have received more than I've given. No, no, you make too much of my help."

"I don't know if I should tell you this." Mrs. Baig cast a look at Mona and then Salamat Ali.

"Do tell us, Mrs. Baig! I'm speaking for Mona as well because she speaks so little. I'm sure she also wants to know."

"Everyone knows I can speak my—" Mona said, but Mrs. Baig didn't let her finish.

"The truth is, from the very first day that Salamat Ali arrived as a tenant at my house, I thought he'd make a wonderful husband for my Mona." Mrs. Baig's tone had changed to a conspiratorial whisper.

Mona looked away to avoid Salamat Ali's gaze. He had been staring at Mona and grinning ever since she smiled at him. Mrs. Baig was chattering away, but neither of them listened. From time to time Salamat Ali's lips parted in a grin and his teeth would show under his moustaches. Once, Mona found the sight so ridiculous that she burst out laughing. Mrs. Baig had just finished recounting how happy she had felt when Mona responded favourably to Salamat Ali's proposal. Hearing her laugh heartily, Mrs. Baig looked hard at her. She probably found it immodest of Mona to flaunt her feelings for Salamat Ali so unashamedly before him. She continued a little tersely, "Well, as I was telling you—"

Salamat Ali must have interpreted Mona's laughter in the same way, because after their return from the hotel, when they were standing outside her house, he caught her hand on the pretext of shaking it.

"I can't tell you how happy I feel, I'm so glad you consented to see me."

Mona felt Salamat Ali's left hand on her wrist. His right hand kept softly pumping hers.

Mrs. Baig had moved a little closer to her own door but did not go inside.

"So what time do you go to bed?" he asked in a longing voice. He spoke softly to avoid being overheard by Mrs. Baig.

"Soon. I mean, not too late," she said, trying unsuccessfully to pull her hand away.

"Really?" He sounded disappointed. He was gazing into her eyes. "I'll be awake until late, thinking—"

He's totally shameless, Mona thought, as her initial happy feelings gave way to dismay.

She saw Mrs. Baig move to get a better view of what was going on. With an effort Mona forced her hand from his grip.

"Thank you, once again, Mrs. Baig!" she said. "It was a very nice evening. Very kind of you to arrange it."

Salamat Ali had his back to Mrs. Baig. He nodded meaningfully to Mona, as he had done on their first encounter.

Mona made sure the bedroom curtains were fully drawn before turning on the lights. Still, when undressing she had a distinct feeling that Salamat Ali was standing on his balcony and could see her naked through the walls. She drifted off to sleep wondering if it was by accident that his leg had rubbed against hers under the table so many times.

And why does he imagine, she thought, that she would let him into her house before the wedding day? She could not think of anything that she had done to encourage him, and decided to be even more careful when she met him at Hina's house. She suddenly felt self-conscious about meeting everyone there in Salamat Ali's presence.

THE FAMILY HAD GATHERED at Hina's house by the time Mrs. Baig and Salamat Ali arrived. Uncle Sajid Mir and Aunt Aneesa had refused to attend. Tanya and Amber were there with their husbands. Faraz's face didn't show any sign of displeasure after the incident with Mrs. Kazi. He had greeted Hina and Jafar in the usual manner and excitedly showed Jafar his new camera. Tanya had already informed Hina that Faraz had not mentioned the subject to her. Hina told Mona that Mrs. Kazi was too humiliated to even mention it to her son.

There were two other distant relatives—one of them an old lady who confused Hina with Mona, and at one point asked Hina why she was marrying another man while Jafar was still alive; the other Umar Shafi, whom Mona tried to avoid.

Umar Shafi was Mona's second cousin on her father's side. He was nine years older than Mona but always maintained that their age difference was only six years. Being the only male member of her father's family other than Uncle Sajid Mir, he was always present at family gatherings. He attended in his trademark navy-blue three-piece suit with large golden buttons that smelled strongly of mothballs. The remnants of his hair had been carefully plastered over the pate. He had recently shaved off his moustaches, which only augmented his bony features and oily look. Umar Shafi had once been interested in Hina, but when she married Jafar he turned his attentions to Mona, who had discouraged him without seemingly affecting his ardour. He had even composed some verses for her. Then Aunt Aneesa had taken charge and decided that Umar Shafi must wed her older daughter on the eve of middle age. Umar Shafi was ready to take the plunge when a worthier suitor arrived and Aunt Aneesa abandoned him without offering any warning, explanation or future hope. At one time Rubab was considered too precious for the likes of Umar

Shafi, but that was in the past, and it was now rumoured that Umar Shafi was interested in her. Many considered the rumour to have been started by Aunt Aneesa herself, but Umar Shafi had neither confirmed nor denied it. It was commonly held that Sajid Mir would give his house to Rubab as her dowry and move into a smaller apartment. It seemed that the carrot was being offered blatantly, because Umar Shafi still rented.

Four days earlier, after receiving the invitation for the gathering, Umar Shafi had phoned Hina and asked her if she knew that Sajid Mir and Aunt Aneesa were against Mona remarrying. Hina told him that it did not matter, because Mona was happy to consider the proposal. Hina was going out with Jafar when he called and had neither the time nor any desire to discuss the reasons for Mona's decision and offer the information about Salamat Ali that Umar Shafi wished to know. Hina wondered for a moment why he seemed so curious, then forgot all about it.

Finally, two days later, Mona received a four-pound cream cake from Umar Shafi, inscribed with the words FOR MONA in condensed strawberry syrup. Mona gave the cake to Noori and Habib to share. She did not wish to become the focus of her cousin's tiresome attentions again. Now she remembered that she had caught Umar Shafi gaping at her a few times on the day of her bereavement. In her grief she had taken no notice of him, nor taken any steps to avoid him. Reminded of it, Mona felt disgust. On two subsequent occasions when he called on her house with additional edible offerings, with Noori's help, Mona suc-cessfully turned Umar Shafi away without seeing him.

Mona had done up her hair in a bun and was wearing an apple-green sari with matching shoes. For the first time in many years she had worn high heels, after trying them on earlier in the morning and making sure that she could still walk in them. When she took them out she was surprised that in all the years that she had had the shoes, she never realized that they perfectly matched this sari. Salamat Ali could not take his eyes off her and stared at her without regard for the guests. Faraz and Kamal exchanged glances and laughed quietly. At one point Amber elbowed Kamal to stop his sniggering.

Upon seeing Salamat Ali, Umar Shafi gave a start.

"Do you two know each other?" Jafar asked, surprised by Umar Shafi's reaction.

"No, I don't think so," he said.

"I can say with certainty that we're meeting for the very first time," Salamat Ali rejoined.

Jafar later told Mona that he found their remarks somewhat disingenuous.

When they were sitting in the drawing room after dinner, Salamat Ali left the room for a few moments to help Jafar load up the tea trolley in the kitchen. Umar Shafi found his chance and sat down very close to Mona on the sofa. The whiff of mothballs became overwhelming.

Umar Shafi looked around and cleared his throat. "There are some silly rumours going around about me and Rubab," he began. "I wanted to put your mind at ease, Mona."

Umar Shafi would have said something more, but Salamat Ali suddenly dropped down onto the sofa right next to him. There was a flash and the click of a camera shutter.

"Thank you very much, Faraz!" Salamat Ali said, taking his arm off Umar Shafi's shoulders. "This will be a keepsake now for both me and Mona. May God always keep Umar Shafi Sahib among us, but when people reach a certain age . . ." He left the sentence unfinished.

Hina burst out laughing. Mona's face grew red as she tried to control her laughter. Umar Shafi was beside himself with rage. Later Amber heard him telling Jafar that Salamat Ali himself did not look a day younger than sixty-five years. Tanya later told Mona that Salamat Ali's comment had been in bad taste.

Hina now took Mona aside into the kitchen and inquired about Umar Shafi. When Mona told her about the cake incident, Hina said, "You should have mentioned that to me! I wouldn't have invited him. It was only because of you that I didn't invite Imad today, although he's in town."

Mona moved away from Hina to pour herself a glass of water from the pitcher on the dining table. "It would have been pointless. You had already sent out the invitations. And what would you have thought if you had heard of it?"

"That my little sister is driving all able-bodied men of the town berserk with desire," Hina said. "Although in Umar Shafi's case, one has really to stretch the definition of able-bodied."

Mona turned to look at Hina and they both laughed.

"I feel embarrassed by all the attention," Mona said. "It makes me uncomfortable. Especially with Tanya and Amber here—"

Hina interrupted her. "Just enjoy your life, okay? You deserve to be happy. And don't think of your daughters as little girls any more. They're both grown up women. Stop worrying about them."

By the end of the evening, both Faraz and Kamal were talking freely and making jokes with Salamat Ali. Hina looked at Jafar, who winked at her. They glanced at Mona, who was regarding her daughters and Salamat Ali in turn with a smile on her face.

On catching sight of Salamat Ali ogling her pedicured feet, which fit nicely in her open-toed shoes, Mona gave up her plans of showing greater modesty in Salamat Ali's presence. Salamat Ali decidedly was not Akbar Ahmad. Why must she punish him for being who he was? She swung her crossed leg a little as she talked to Amber. The gathering was turning out to be a greater success than she had hoped.

"Everything went well for you?" Hina later asked Mona.

She nodded. Salamat Ali was coming towards them.

When Mrs. Baig and Salamat Ali took their leave, Hina stood next to Mona. Salamat Ali appeared to know his boundaries. When shaking hands with Mona, he let her draw away her hand after giving it just a little squeeze.

IN THE FOLLOWING DAYS, the servants began smiling shyly at Salamat Ali. Mona heard loud greetings when they sighted him going in or out of Mrs. Baig's house. Once while complaining to Mona about her good-for-nothing husband, Noori said, "He doesn't take care of me at all. Look at Salamat Sahib now. How nicely he treats you."

"Really!" Mona said with mock surprise.

"Yes, the other day he told Habib, the gardener and me that if we kept you happy we'll all get a twenty per cent raise in our salaries on your wedding and all of us will also get cloth for a dress."

"I guess you will." Mona smiled.

"He also promised me that you'll buy me a nose ring made of one hundred per cent pure silver. Will you really, Mona bibi?"

Mona nodded.

"I want a husband just like him," Noori said.

That evening, Mona received a letter from Salamat Ali in which he wrote that he had run into unexpected opposition from his family to the idea of his marrying a widow. He wrote that he did not care whether or not they attended to bless the ceremony, for now he had her, and nothing else mattered.

The reaction from Salamat Ali's family only confirmed Mona's view that while a widow who seeks a second marriage was looked down upon as a harlot in society, widowers were expected to look for virgin brides.

Mona felt a sudden surge of affection for Salamat Ali.

AS THE MARRIAGE was the second one for both parties, and both were at a certain stage in their lives, they dispensed with the usual razzle-dazzle and the many rituals leading up to the wedding ceremony. Hina had suggested that instead of holding two individual receptions on behalf of the bride and the bridegroom, they should have a joint reception. It was also decided that the marriage ceremony would be held at Hina's house. Salamat Ali had acceded to the decisions. He had requested only to be allowed to choose the caterers for the occasion. "People remember a wedding by the meal they had at the reception," he told Hina when she discussed the menu with him. "It is too important a matter to be left to chance."

As Mona and Hina completed the list of invitees, Mrs. Baig complained that the preparations looked too lacklustre.

"We should avoid any immodest extremes of happiness on the occasion," Hina told her while looking at Mona, "so that we are not seen as rubbing salt into the wounds of the relatives."

Mona nodded. She did not wish to attract too much attention on the occasion. As well, she had to consider the feelings of her daughters. Amber had dropped by several times to help her with small chores, but Tanya had not visited recently. Amber told Mona that Tanya was too busy at work.

"They will have to come to terms with your marriage eventually," Hina said to Mona. "The more solemn we make it, the sooner things will be normalized in the family."

At Salamat Ali's request, Mrs. Baig took Mona to choose a sari to wear for the ceremony. Mona had earlier turned down Salamat Ali's request that she wear a traditional bridal dress. "Can't you see how ridiculous I would look sitting in a red bridal dress with married daughters and grandchildren of my own?" she told Mrs. Baig. Still, Mrs. Baig did not concede without grumbling.

In the end, Mona chose an olive-green georgette sari with a scalloped border and a matching blouse with intricate sequin-work.

The bride's family was supposed to provide the bridegroom's dress. Hina asked Salamat Ali if he had any preference between a suit and a *sherwani*.

"I am leaving everything to Mona's discretion," he told her. "Let her decide."

Mona and Hina consulted and decided that a *sherwani* would look better on him for the occasion.

Mona had not counted on Salamat Ali wearing a *patka* on the wedding day. Amber and Hina laughed loudly when they saw Salamat Ali enter, sporting a golden silk *patka* on his head, a screen of tassels hanging over his face.

Faraz insisted that Salamat Ali keep on the headgear until the end of the reception.

"Don't worry," Salamat Ali said with a wink, leaning towards him. "It's the last thing I will take off tonight." Then, putting the *patka* askew on his head, he added roguishly, "A *patka* is to a bridegroom what a mane is to a lion."

The ceremony was held in the garden where a sofa set was placed for the bride, bridegroom and a few close relatives. Chairs were arranged in a semicircle in front of the sofa for the guests. Nearly fifty people attended. Hina and Jafar had invited several of their friends. Hina and Jafar's son and daughter-in-law had also come down from Islamabad for the occasion. There were also some distant relatives of Salamat Ali's and a few of his business acquaintances. One of Jafar's uncles read the wedding sermon, after which the papers were signed, witnessed and sent for registration.

Salamat Ali had prayed with great fervour when the wedding sermon was read. As soon as the sermon was over,

Salamat Ali got up and made a sign to the caterer who had arranged the food tables at the far end of the garden in an open tent. At Salamat Ali's signal, he lit the kerosene lamps under the serving dishes and started warming the food. Half an hour later, at another signal from Salamat Ali, the meal was served. Salamat Ali looked and nodded to Jafar every time someone praised the food.

During the ceremony, Umar Shafi stared at Salamat Ali with malicious intent. Mrs. Kazi never stopped whispering to Faraz.

Uncle Sajid Mir and Aunt Aneesa boycotted the event, along with their older daughter. Mona felt hurt because when Aunt Aneesa's older daughter had gotten married, Mona, although pregnant with Tanya, had embroidered all the clothes for her dowry. Aunt Aneesa had sent Rubab in the hope that she might yet catch the eye of a prospective suitor. Rubab wore a glittering red dress and her layer of makeup was thicker than ever. Later, in looking at the wedding photos, Mona noticed that Rubab appeared in every group shot taken, striking her signature meek pose. Three days later, Salamat Ali moved his belongings into Mona's house. Mona put his bedding away in the storage room and made room in the bathroom for his toiletries, hair-colouring kit and the two large bottles of hair oil. Mona was surprised to see a cookbook among Salamat Ali's things. It seemed well used. In a small cardboard box that Salamat Ali carefully put on top of the cupboard, Mona found a pair of binoculars. She went to the window and looked through them at Mrs. Baig's balcony. The flowers seemed so close she could almost touch them. Mona quickly removed the

binoculars from her eyes. She realized why she had sometimes felt that Salamat Ali was watching her.

Salamat Ali soon settled in. When Mona brought him
shaving water she found that he had already shaved with
tap water. He took out his own clothes for work and put
them on in no particular order. Mona also noticed that he
did not care how long the tea had been steeped. As he was
the sole owner of his paper distribution agency, he kept
hours of his choice. He often came home for lunch.
Sometimes he stayed late at work and when he returned he
did not immediately go to sleep. Mona began going to bed
later and later. The servants received what Salamat Ali had
promised them. Habib, the gardener, Noori and the washerwoman stood in a line while he handed out Mona's gifts. All
the servants felt very important and were duly impressed by
the solemnity Salamat Ali bestowed on the occasion.

VI

THE PORTRAIT

A week after the wedding cer-
emony, Hina and Jafar brought over all the wedding gifts
that had been stored at their house since that night. They
had dinner with Mona and Salamat Ali and stayed up till
late.

The following morning, the house was quiet when Mona
woke up and came down to make tea. Habib had taken a day
off and Noori was to come later in the day. Mona was in the
kitchen taking out the cups and saucers from the crockery
cabinet when she heard footsteps behind her and Salamat
Ali's arms circled her waist. His lips pressed against her
neck. He turned her to face him.

"Not here!" Mona said.

"There's nobody in the house."

"Still—"

He kissed her.

"I'm just finishing making the tea," Mona said.

"Let me make the tea for you today."

"No, no, it's improper. Let me do it."

"Never!" Salamat Ali said. "You should go and sit comfortably in the living room. I'll bring tea to you there myself. It will be ready in no time."

Mona remained restless until she had made certain Salamat Ali knew where he would find all the tea things. Finally, she turned to go.

"Mona!" Salamat Ali said.

"Hmm—" As she turned she felt Salamat Ali's hand on her hips.

She caught his hand as it began sliding down. "You were going to make the tea."

"Okay." he laughed. "Okay."

She still felt his eyes on her body.

She picked up a gift bow that had come unstuck from one of the gift boxes piled up on the living room sofa. Akbar Ahmad had kept a close watch over the gift boxes since their delivery. Mona wondered if he questioned the contents; she saw him looking down with curiosity. Mona remembered how decades ago he had spent a good part of their wedding night opening gifts and making a detailed inventory of who had given what gift, listing its approximate value on a notepad.

Mona picked up the phone and dialled Hina's number. Hina and Jafar had invited them to breakfast at the hotel today. Mona was to call when they were ready so that Hina and Jafar could come and pick them up.

"You sound strange," Hina said. "Are you okay? I hope you haven't forgotten that we're going out for breakfast."

"Of course I'm okay," Mona said self-consciously, as she looked away from Akbar Ahmad's portrait.

Hina was laughing at the other end. "Wake up now and be ready in half an hour."

As Mona said goodbye and hung up the phone, she heard Salamat Ali bringing in the teacups and quickly stood up.

"Let us have tea in the garden," she said.

"As you wish," he answered.

Mona let him pass through the door first. Before she stepped out, she quickly turned her head to glance at Akbar Ahmad's portrait.

The house had been repainted a few days before the wedding ceremony. The painters had not removed the portrait from the wall; when they painted around it, they left paint smudges on the wooden frame. Mona had not had a chance to clean it yet. Mona wondered if Akbar Ahmad's portrait looked bigger than usual because of the newly painted wall.

"FARAZ'S MOTHER WANTS TO invite you and Salamat Ali for dinner," Tanya told Mona over the phone. "She's been bothering Faraz since she found out that we took you out for dinner to a hotel. She didn't believe we met accidentally. She said she knew very well what was going on."

Hina had told Tanya to make sure that Mrs. Kazi was kept in the dark the first time she and Faraz invited Mona and Salamat Ali out for dinner, to make sure that there was no unpleasantness.

"Mrs. Kazi is welcome to her opinions, Tanya." Mona said.

"You know what she said today?"

"I'm holding my breath."

"She said that she's not your enemy. That Aunt Hina was the one who twisted her words to pick a fight. She said that she had nothing against you or else she wouldn't have attended the wedding."

"I don't want to start discussing all that. I'll let you know about the dinner in a few days, Tanya," Mona said, and then put down the phone.

Later, when Hina called her, Mona told her about Mrs. Kazi's invitation.

"The enemy has decided to mend bridges to pave the way for future offensives," Hina said.

"I thought so, too, and I'm concerned. Salamat Ali doesn't come across as someone quick to take offence, but he knows of the opposition to his proposal from the family. Any caustic remarks by Mrs. Kazi wouldn't go over well with him."

"I think you'll have to go. It would look bad to delay it for too long. Salamat Ali can equally take offence at Tanya's family giving him the cold shoulder, you know. You certainly don't want to aggravate the situation there. In any event, sooner or later he has to meet the marvel that is Tanya's mother-in-law."

Mona finally called Tanya to accept the invitation for the following Sunday.

She had told Salamat Ali in passing that Mrs. Kazi was "quite a character."

"I can't wait to meet her," Salamat Ali said.

~~~

ON THE DAY of Mrs. Kazi's dinner invitation, Mona was putting away the dishes in the kitchen when she saw the gardener open the gate and Salamat Ali drive up in a beige car. She came out, shading her eyes from the sun with her hand, as Salamat Ali walked up to her smiling.

"Did you buy it?" Mona asked, as he jingled the keys in her face.

"For you!"

"But I don't drive."

"That was why you married me."

"Are you sure that was the reason?" Mona smiled.

"I've yet to find another good one. Unless, of course"—Salamat Ali quickly looked around—"you'd like to provide me with one right now."

"Don't you dare attempt anything here," Mona said. "The gardener is watching."

Mona had never guessed that Salamat Ali intended to buy a car, but she felt neither surprised nor upset that Salamat Ali had not informed her. She had noticed he had an easy way with money and casually bought things on impulse. Salamat Ali had bought a reconditioned model, which he told her had been offered to him at a bargain. Mona was glad she no longer had to wait for Tanya or Amber to take her out shopping. She had often felt that she was imposing on them, but she could not handle Karachi's wild traffic. She had planned to learn to drive several times after Akbar Ahmad's death, but had given up the idea each time when she saw how recklessly people drove in the city streets. She was also conscious of what Akbar Ahmad had told her once when she expressed her desire to learn to drive. *With your habit of day dreaming, you'll crash the car the very first day, for sure.*

They drove to Mrs. Kazi's house in the new car. On the way, Mona kept wondering how long it would have taken Akbar Ahmad to make the decision about purchasing a car. He thought and mulled about even small purchases for many days, sometimes even weeks, and agonized over the decision until the misery became too much for him to endure. Mona had often felt that the decision finally to purchase something was driven as much by the desire to put an end to the constant vexation of worrying about it as it was by its necessity. Any joy that a new purchase might have brought was always absent from the experience.

Mrs. Kazi received Mona and Salamat Ali cordially. Salamat Ali took Tanya's son, Zain, into his arms.

"He looks just like you," he said to Mrs. Kazi. "I saw the resemblance on the wedding day but didn't get a chance to tell you."

"Really?' Mrs. Kazi threw a quick glance at Tanya.

"Of course! The boy is your exact copy. The same nose, the same naughty twinkle in the eyes."

Tanya laughed despite herself. Mona tried not to.

Unable to make out what Salamat Ali really meant, Mrs. Kazi focused her attention on Mona. It was a glance that sought iniquity in her every little gesture, in every hint of expression on her face. Mona was wearing a simple white sari with a blue embroidered border. Mrs. Kazi looked at it and nodded grudgingly. Mona felt grateful for Hina's advice to dress simply that day.

"Speaking of looks, Mrs. Kazi, don't you think Mona is looking stunning today?" Salamat Ali asked, putting down Zain.

"Yes, yes." Mrs. Kazi tried to walk away.

"No, Mrs. Kazi, tell me the truth now. Take a *good* look at her and give me your honest opinion. Wouldn't you say that Mona has never looked prettier?"

"As you say, as you say. Yes, yes," Mrs. Kazi said with exasperation.

Mona pinched Salamat Ali when no one was looking.

But even in the face of Salamat Ali's pre-emption, Mrs. Kazi did not give up. When they entered the drawing room, she sat down next to Salamat Ali and looked him over as if measuring him. To avoid any possible attention to herself, Amber sat far away from Mrs. Kazi. "I'm so happy that our Mona has found some support for this part of her life," Mrs. Kazi said, while Tanya served samosas and papads. "We had always thought that Tanya and Amber's father would remain with us forever, but there's no knowing what fate has ordained for us."

"True! True!" Salamat Ali said, reaching for a samosa.

Mona glanced uneasily at her daughters. Tanya put down the snacks plate and sat down opposite her mother. Her expression had hardened. Mona felt disappointed in her all of a sudden. It was to oblige Tanya that she had accepted Mrs. Kazi's invitation.

Mrs. Kazi addressed Salamat Ali. "I heard that your first wife, too . . ."

"Yes, some years ago," Salamat Ali said. "It was a fortunate accident for me to find Mona."

"It's become much easier these days to find people who think alike, hasn't it?" Mrs. Kazi said. "In our times it was very difficult. In fact, in good families it was considered very scandalous at one time to marry after one's spouse died. Especially for women. And some consider it very disreputable still."

"Mummy, aren't we going to have some tea?" Faraz asked nervously. Mrs. Kazi ignored him, and Tanya turned away. Appearing rather foolish as nobody answered or looked at him, Faraz picked up Zain, who had been playing on the floor, and went into the kitchen.

"What you say is absolutely true, Mrs. Kazi." Salamat Ali watched Faraz leave the room. "But the virtue of self-denial is given only to a few. Like yourself."

"What do you mean?" Mrs. Kazi stared at Salamat Ali.

"What I mean is, you proved resolute in the face of temptation. I salute you."

"What temptation?" Mrs. Kazi now looked suspiciously at Salamat Ali. "What are you talking about?"

"Oh, you are too modest, Mrs. Kazi! You understand perfectly what I mean."

"No, I don't. What is it?" Mrs. Kazi said guardedly, darting a quick glance at Mona for any signs of conspiracy against her.

Mona was eyeing Salamat Ali, wondering what he alluded to.

"Mr. Kazi died when—seven, eight years ago?" Salamat Ali asked, looking at Mrs. Kazi.

"That's right!" Mrs. Kazi sat up stiffly.

"Ah, such self-denial. Such self-denial."

"Would you finally say what you mean?" Mrs. Kazi's agitation was growing.

"Well, Mrs. Kazi." Salamat Ali spoke slowly, a strange smile playing on his face. "If you could make men turn their heads now, I can well imagine how many men you would have killed with your looks then."

"*What?*"

The silence after Mrs. Kazi's exclamation was so complete that Mona could clearly hear Tanya gulp. Mona looked at Amber, who was staring at Salamat Ali with mouth open.

Mrs. Kazi glanced at Mona and then quickly composed herself.

"No, no, Mrs. Kazi." Salamat Ali wagged his finger knowingly, "Don't look so surprised. I saw everything at our wedding ceremony. Oh yes, I saw how the men looked at you."

Amber had overcome her shock at Salamat Ali's words and it seemed that she would burst out laughing at any moment. Mona gave her an admonishing look. Amber turned away.

"Oh, you are too much, Salamat Ali Sahib!" Mrs. Kazi finally said, throwing a triumphant glance at Mona.

Mona who had exercised great self-control to hold back her own laughter finally let go. She admired the dexterity with which Salamat Ali had changed the whole complexion of the conversation. He had not been mistaken in his reading of Mrs. Kazi. Tanya, who had lowered her head so that no one would notice that her face had become red in trying to hide the smile on her face, called out, "Do you need any help, Faraz?" Then, without waiting for an answer, she got up and went into the kitchen.

Mrs. Kazi had been completely sidetracked, and now looked thoughtful and nervous. Salamat Ali was helping himself to the papads. When Mrs. Kazi was not looking, he winked at Mona.

"I'd forgotten to ask what you like to eat," Mrs. Kazi said to Salamat Ali, tucking her hair into her bun with a nervous gesture.

"Anything made by your hand will be a delight," Salamat Ali said. "Right, Mona?"

"Of course!" Mona replied heartily.

"Since I had my cataract removed, I avoid cooking as much as I can," Mrs. Kazi said, glancing uneasily towards Mona.

Mona could see that she again felt some anxiety about the motive behind Salamat Ali's comments.

"When did that happen?" Salamat Ali asked in a concerned tone, taking a big bite of the papad.

"Oh, many years ago," Mrs. Kazi replied, getting up.

"I'd like to hear all about it," Salamat Ali said, and followed Mrs. Kazi into the kitchen.

Tanya came out of the kitchen as the two entered.

The rest of the evening Mrs. Kazi was excessively polite towards both Salamat Ali and Mona. And for the first time Mona was enjoying herself at Mrs. Kazi's house.

After dinner everyone went to the drawing room, where tea was served. Salamat Ali liked the strong blend, praising the tea so effusively that Tanya had to get up and bring him a second cup.

After finishing it, Salamat Ali turned towards Mona, squeezed her knee in view of everyone and said, "Shall we go?"

Mona was mortified. She saw Mrs. Kazi witness the act with a look of mingled shock and satisfaction. Mona saw her turn to Faraz and say something, and Tanya flushed. Salamat Ali had left his hand on her knee. Rather than pushing his hand away, which would have made this more awkward for her, Mona got up from her place and took Zain into her arms.

"I'm ready," she said.

She was most concerned about what Tanya and Amber would think. Even their husbands did not take physical liberties with them before the family.

THE FIFTH BIRTHDAY reception of Amber's daughter, Maha, was to be held at Mona's. Tanya dropped by that afternoon and announced happily that Mrs. Kazi would not attend.

"Everything okay?" Mona asked.

"In the morning as Faraz was taking us to the hair salon, she rushed out of the veranda to beat me to the front seat of the car and *crash!*" Tanya said gleefully. "She twisted her foot on a loose paving stone in the driveway."

Salamat Ali came out of the kitchen where he was serving himself. "What happened, Tanya?" he asked.

"Just an accident. Mrs. Kazi sprained her ankle," Mona answered, seeing Tanya purse her lips with annoyance.

"Very sad! Very sad!" Salamat Ali kept mixing the rice and curry with his hands. "I really like your mother-in-law, Tanya."

Tanya continued to speak to Mona without looking at him. She was no longer in a cheerful mood.

AFTER TANYA HAD LEFT, Salamat Ali winked at Mona and said, "I'm sorry to hear that Mrs. Kazi won't be there. Now you can wear something more lively. There will only be Tanya, Amber, and Hina and her husband."

"And Faraz and Kamal."

"They'll be proud to see what a sexy mother-in-law they have."

"Don't be so shameless!" Mona blushed. She opened the trunk to look for something suitable to wear.

"What is that sari there?" Salamat Ali had caught sight of the Banarasi sari lying folded in the back of the trunk.

It was the sari Akbar Ahmad had given Mona.

In the early years of their marriage, after Akbar Ahmad got his first promotion, Mona often thought of putting away some money every month to buy herself a Banarasi sari. She had considered wearing one to family gatherings and parties, but Akbar Ahmad, who handled the household budget, explained to her that other, more urgent expenses would not leave any money to be put away. He persisted with his rational explanations of household needs until Mona felt guilty at the thought of indulging in extravagances like Banarasi saris. Then, many years later, on the occasion of their Silver Jubilee, Akbar Ahmad had surprised her with the gift of this sari. When Mona pressed him to find out what had made him think of it, he confessed that he himself had been at a loss about what to get for her. Tanya had bought it on his behalf because she knew her mother's taste better. A few months ago, Mona had removed the sari from the trunk where she kept it. She loved the colours. The turquoise sari had an embroidered floral border embellished with silver-leaf and sequins. She had even made herself a turquoise blouse in satin with silver piping, but now she felt self-conscious at the very thought of putting it on. She considered herself to be past the age of dressing in such youthful colours. Akbar Ahmad had probably forgotten all about it the day after he gave it to her, since he never once asked her to wear it for him. She had often thought of giving the sari to Tanya.

"That's too flashy!" Mona said to Salamat Ali, and tried to close the trunk.

"Put it on, put it on. Let me see!"

Mona reluctantly unfolded the sari and held it up to herself while looking in the mirror. She stood there for a moment, thinking. The sari suited her.

"That's it! You must wear it this evening," Salamat Ali said.

"But—"

"No ifs, ands or buts!" Salamat Ali picked up the plate in which he was mixing the hair dye. "And from now on, no more of Hina telling you what to wear. It's a conspiracy. They're all jealous of you."

Mona regarded Salamat Ali silently. He was looking in the mirror, whistling to himself as he applied the colour to his hair.

"Let me do it," Mona said, picking up the plate with the dye. "Give me the brush, Salamat."

~~~

"MY GOD, YOU LOOK *SO* PRETTY!" Hina said the moment she entered. Just then, Tanya and Jafar also walked in and stopped to look. Tanya came closer.

"Isn't that the same sari that—" she began.

"Yes, it is," Mona said sharply.

"Which sari?" Salamat Ali asked, turning to Mona, but Amber hastily changed the subject.

Later, there was a general discussion of how the children should address Salamat Ali.

"What about Uncle Salamat?" Kamal said.

"You can address me as Uncle if you want, Kamal," Salamat Ali said. "But if the children call their grandmother Nani, I should be called Nana. Isn't that right, Maha?"

Amber's daughter Maha was too busy admiring her own sequined dress to answer. She quietly nodded when it was agreed among the adults that the children would address Salamat Ali as Nana. But now, as the child was carried past Akbar Ahmad's portrait, Maha recalled that there had been another Nana not long ago. She pointed her finger at the portrait and said loudly, "Nana!"

Everyone turned to look.

"Yes," Salamat Ali replied. "Nana."

"And you?" the child asked.

Salamat Ali pointed the finger at his own face and said, "New Nana!" Then he put his finger on the portrait and said, "Old Nana!"

Maha seemed to accept the change in guard, for she did not say anything more.

Amber, Kamal and Mona all appeared relieved.

"I keep forgetting to ask you," Hina said, when she found Mona alone for a moment. "What is Akbar Ahmad doing hanging there like a naked sword over poor Salamat Ali's head? I never thought you were so morbid."

Mona did not answer. She usually avoided looking at the portrait, but every time it caught attention, it seemed to have grown a little bigger. Hina also kept quiet seeing that Mona was unwilling to discuss the subject.

At the dining table, Salamat Ali piled food on Mona's plate. Tanya watched them from the corner of her eye.

When Salamat Ali served Mona another chicken leg, Tanya asked her, "Have you been for your quarterly checkup lately?"

"Yes, just last week. Everything was clear." Then, turning to Salamat Ali she said, "No more please, Salamat. You have some now."

"I say we should eat as much as we can, Tanya," Salamat Ali said. "We're old people, you know. We could take off at any time. We should enjoy life while we're here. What do you say, Faraz? Kamal?"

"With all that black hair, Mr. Salamat Ali, who can dare say that you are old," Kamal replied.

"Our Kamal speaks very little, Amber," Salamat Ali was not embarrassed. "But when he speaks he scores. Just for that, a nice breast for you, Kamal." Salamat Ali ladled one onto his plate. "Don't refuse. Who doesn't like breasts?"

Tanya looked away.

Salamat Ali took charge of serving the desserts. After clearing the table, he laid out the platter of sweetmeats and put a gulab jaman into Mona's mouth. She brought her hand up but did not take the gulab jaman from him. She took a bite.

"Jafar, what are you staring at?" Hina said. "I just realized that God has given you two hands, as well."

Making a show of innocence Jafar picked up a gulab jaman and offered it to Mona. Hina slapped his hand.

Kamal, Faraz and Salamat Ali laughed. Mona's face was flushed. She suddenly noticed Amber and Tanya staring at her from the window above the breakfast bar.

The family stayed until around midnight. Just as Mona finished tidying up the living room where Salamat Ali lay sprawled on the sofa, the phone rang. It was Tanya, and she was sobbing.

"What's wrong?" Mona asked.

"You never wore that sari when Daddy was alive," Tanya said.

Before Mona could think of an answer, Tanya had hung up.

Akbar Ahmad's portrait again held Mona's gaze. His presence had never loomed so large in the house, even when he was alive.

Salamat Ali stood up. "Who was it?" he asked, nuzzling Mona's neck.

Mona did not answer. A sense of modesty kept her from mentioning Tanya's name before the man who was undressing her. Salamat Ali did not seem to care. Mona pulled the end of her sari from his hands.

When she turned to leave the room, Salamat Ali cast a brazen glance at Akbar Ahmad's portrait, and gyrating his hips in a vulgar fashion, followed her up the stairs.

VII

A NIGHT AT THE BEACH

On a Friday night, Salamat Ali
returned home later than usual. He seemed pleased with
himself. For some days, he had kept long hours in the midst
of concluding an overseas distribution deal. The time zone
difference kept him working late, he had told Mona.

"Get the tiffin ready for tomorrow morning. I've received
an advance for setting up the network. We're going to the
beach."

"To celebrate?" Mona smiled.

"Yes, to celebrate!" he beamed. "I've booked a beach
house for the whole day. I'll finally make the kebab rolls
I promised."

Mona smelled alcohol on Salamat Ali's breath that day
for the first time. Akbar Ahmad never drank nor served
alcohol at his house, but Mona had learned to countenance
the practice in her family because both Jafar and Faraz
drank socially. Thus far, they had not served alcohol in

Salamat Ali's presence, perhaps, Mona thought, because they felt he might take offence. Now she could let Hina know that Salamat Ali was himself a drinker.

WHEN THEY ARRIVED at the beach house after an hour-long drive, Mona checked out the place. It was spacious but sparsely furnished. However, the rooms were clean and well-aired, and the bedsheets and pillowcases had been freshly changed. Mona was pleased to see the kitchen well stocked and the fridge working. She put the drinking water she had brought into the fridge.

Early that morning Salamat Ali had gone to the meat market to get minced beef for the kebabs. He had also bought some chicken, which he now put in the fridge to marinate for dinner. Then he cooked the kebabs on the coal-grill on the deck and warmed the parathas. Mona offered to help but he would not let her touch anything.

"Just sit down next to me and watch," he said.

They heard the blast of a freighter's horn as it passed in the distance. Then the beach was quiet except for the cries of seabirds and the gentle splashing of waves.

Mona loved the sea. Before Amber's birth, she had often dragged Akbar Ahmad to the beach. He had always gone reluctantly. As time went on, she found it too taxing to persuade him to accompany her and the girls. More recently, she had visited the beach a few times with Amber's and Tanya's families and had enjoyed herself. But right now she felt happier here than she ever had. She was almost glad there weren't too many people at the beach today.

The kebabs were tasty. Afterwards, Mona feared she had overeaten.

When she asked if they were from his cookbook, Salamat Ali replied, "This is a family recipe, madam!"

"Will you give it to me?"

"For the right price." He moistened his lips.

"Salamat."

"Yes?" He stopped, wiped his hands and looked at her.

"What do you see in an old woman like me?"

"Mona!"

"Come, tell me." She pressed his hands against her face.

"I wouldn't know where to begin."

"Be serious now, answer me."

Salamat Ali ignored her question and started touching her. "Maybe here, or here! No, here. Yes! Yes!"

"Stop it!" Mona pushed him away, laughing. "You're tickling me!"

He did not stop, and Mona had to run out of the kitchen. He followed her out onto the sand. They startled a seagull.

Mona suddenly felt embarrassed being out in the open. Although there was nobody on the beach at this hour, she felt too self-conscious to take another step. One of Salamat Ali's sandals came off as he ran to catch up with her. Laughing, he pulled her back into the beach house. Her sandals were filled with sand.

Later, they went for a walk along the beach. Salamat Ali insisted they climb a dune to see the ships in the distance. After the short climb, Mona was out of breath.

"Just a couple more steps," Salamat Ali said. "A few more. Almost there now."

Finally they reached the summit. The view of the horizon was no better from the top of the dune. They tried to look through the haze but could make out only the outlines of the tankers and merchant ships anchored far away.

"Tired?" he asked.

"I haven't climbed in a long while," Mona said, tucking behind her ear a strand of windblown hair.

"What are you thinking?" he asked.

"When I was a little girl, I used to climb trees, you know. We had a mango tree in our garden and I could climb it easily and pick unripe mangoes. Most boys couldn't do it. They usually threw stones to knock down the fruit."

"And did you also shoot at birds with a slingshot?" he teased.

Mona suddenly laughed at their pointless exercise in climbing up the dune.

"What are you laughing at, huh?"

"Nothing."

"Nothing? Really? Well, then nothing is fine with me!"

They sat there for some time, looking around but unable to see much.

Then Salamat Ali started whistling.

"Getting bored?" Mona asked.

"No! No!"

"Let's go."

"No, if you want we can sit here a little longer."

But Mona had already stood up.

He held her hand as they climbed down the slope. She leaned against him.

When they returned to the beach house Mona was aware

of a buoyant feeling that she had not experienced since childhood. It was a quiet happiness. Only after she felt it did she realize how much she had missed it.

Salamat Ali had lighted the coal-grill again. Mona joined him. Before he began roasting the chicken for dinner, Salamat Ali handed Mona a cup.

"What is this? No. This is alcohol. I don't drink."

"Just a drop of scotch—"

Salamat Ali's breath smelled strongly of liquor.

"—take a sip!"

She realized he must have drunk some inside when he took out the chicken. Mona took a sip.

"No more!" she said. "It's too bitter."

"Finish it. Only a little is left in your cup."

Mona drank it. Her nose tingled. She sneezed a few times. By the time Salamat Ali finished roasting, Mona had already laid the table inside. She was still feeling dizzy but it was a pleasant feeling. A cooler breeze had picked up.

During dinner, Salamat Ali caught her hand and pressed it to his heart. "I'm blessed, Mona, truly blessed."

His voice sounded dramatic, and Mona thought it was the effect of the alcohol. She could see a change coming upon Salamat Ali as he drank.

"I never hoped to find a woman with whom I could find true happiness, and now I've found her. Now I've found you."

He repeated those words as he finished off a chicken leg.

"What about your wife? Your first wife? I mean, what was she like?" Mona felt a pang of jealousy and embarrassment on broaching the subject. It was the first time she had brought it up. Salamat Ali had never asked her anything about her life with Akbar Ahmad nor shown the least interest in finding out about him. Whatever opinion he had formulated about her life with Akbar Ahmad he had kept to himself.

"The kindest soul," Salamat Ali said, playing with Mona's fingers. "She'll go straight to heaven."

"How long were you married?"

"Twelve, no, fourteen years!"

"Did she think about having children?" she asked.

"She did." Salamat Ali took a draught of his scotch. "Oh yes, she did! And that was what killed her. The doctors had told her that despite the treatment there was no certainty, but she never gave up hope. She took all kinds of medications. Both prescribed and unprescribed. The pharmacies give out whatever one asks for. There're no regulations. Her body reacted to one of her medicines. There were some further complications too. Her condition kept deteriorating after that. Poor soul."

"I'm sorry," Mona said, regretting she had brought up the subject.

"We visited every clinic," Salamat Ali carried on. "Then every *pir* and *faqir* and magician. All to no avail."

She finally asked the question that had preyed on her mind. "Did *you* miss not having children?"

"In the beginning I did. But when I realized that it was the will of God, I endured it quietly. She didn't accept it, though. I told her we could adopt a child, but she wanted to have one of our own."

"How long was she sick?"

"More than two years. My business suffered. It was a hard time. For the first year she was kept at home, but as her condition kept worsening, I moved her to a hospital. I left home early, visited her on my way to work, then went from work straight to the hospital. And yet she was still bitter."

"Bitter? Bitter about what?" Mona asked.

"Bitter, very bitter, There were no thanks. I did the best I could. It was fate."

Mona did not know what kind of relationship Salamat Ali had had with his first wife. She could only judge it from the experience of her relationship with him.

As she listened to Salamat Ali describe how he cared for his wife for the two years of her illness, she discovered that his wife was young at the time of her death—not more than forty-two or forty-three. Mona realized she was now nearly ten years older than his wife had been when she died. When sick herself Mona never allowed attendants or care-takers, because it reminded her of the days of her mother's illness. But now part of her wished she would fall sick and have Salamat Ali by her side—feeding her porridge, administering medicine, helping her sit up, cutting and peeling fruit for her.

"What is past is past," Salamat Ali said. "Now I have you. Enough of all this sadness and grief. Sit here close to me. Let me feel your body by my side. What a beautiful night. Isn't it?"

Mona felt his manner somewhat indelicate, given the subject of their conversation, but she sat down next to him. Salamat Ali poured some more scotch for himself. Absentmindedly he poured some for Mona as well. She did not have the heart to stop him. As he continued drinking he forced Mona to keep him company. Trying not to smell the drink, she swallowed it in bigger than usual draughts. Soon she felt dizzy and her eyes kept closing. When she opened them next she saw Salamat Ali walking with a wavering gait towards the car. A few days remained before the night of the full moon but already the tide had a turbulent energy and the noise of crashing waves rose steadily. A feeling of bliss slowly spread through Mona's body, making her forget everything else.

But then she saw Salamat Ali open the trunk of the car and take out a CD player. He brought it to the deck after plugging it to an extension cord. He was playing a *ghazal* collection. Mona thought the volume was too loud.

"Come, let's go into the water," he said.

"No, I'm too dizzy to walk. It's dangerous," Mona said.

"Take my hand." Salamat Ali began dragging her.

"No, I can't!" she protested. "Let go of me, Salamat. Let me go! Someone will see, Salamat."

He slung her over his shoulder and wobbled unsteadily towards the water. She finally managed to get down, but in the struggle he lost his balance and fell. In trying to keep him upright, she fell over too. Both of them broke out laughing.

Suddenly Salamat Ali stopped laughing and looked around him in a daze. "Where is everyone?"

"There's nobody here, Salamat," Mona said. "We're by ourselves."

"No, no, no! There're all these beach houses around here. There must be someone in them." He crawled on his hands and knees a little way towards one and picked up a stone.

"HOY!" he shouted as he flung the stone at the beach house.

Mona heard the sound of glass breaking.

"Son of a whore! Who was that?" The shout came from the guard's post on the street. "Just you wait!"

Salamat Ali laughed and bent down to pick up another stone, but Mona got up to pull him away before the guard arrived.

"No, no, no! They're inside, I know!" Salamat Ali said, holding on to her for support. "They'll come out now!"

"Enough, Salamat! Stop it!" Mona said, and led him away.

They came inside the beach house where Mona washed the sand from his feet with warm water. Mona made him coffee, and after drinking it and eating a piece of lime, he seemed to feel much better. Mona had been upset about his behaviour, but she laughed now when she saw him warming his hands around the coffee mug and winking at her. Mona thought about what he had said about his wife being unable to conceive. She wondered if Salamat Ali sometimes acted so childishly because he had never been a father himself.

She walked up to him. They kissed.

"So you forgive me?" he whispered, looking strangely at her.

"Don't be foolish. What's there to forgive?" Mona was wondering if it was the drink that made her kiss so audaciously.

"I love you so much," Salamat Ali said with half-closed eyes, pulling Mona towards the bed.

As Mona helped him into bed, he suddenly pulled her on top of him.

"And here I was worried that you had drunk too much," she said with a smile.

Salamat Ali rolled over. It was dark and Mona could see only his silhouette as he leaned over her.

They heard the guard blast his whistle at regular intervals. He was making his rounds after an unsuccessful search for the culprit who had thrown the stone.

SALAMAT ALI TOOK MONA with him to help him in shopping for a wedding gift for his broker's daughter. He said that it would be a good occasion to return the man's past favours. After driving around for fifteen minutes on Tariq Road, Salamat Ali was unable to find a shady spot to park the car. Finally he parked in the sun and they walked into the mall.

"It's so hot today. Let me know when you're ready for lunch," he said to Mona.

As they passed the jeweller's shop, Salamat Ali stopped and said to her, "Let's go inside and cool off a bit."

After a few minutes inside, however, Mona began to feel chilly. The big air conditioners, which whirred softly, had made it too cold. But she admired a gold *nau-ratan* set. The salesman brought it out of the showcase and adjusted the angle of the pedestal mirror so that she could hold it up to her neck. Salamat Ali stood next to her.

"You won't find this workmanship anywhere else in the market," the salesman said. "Our father has made it. He doesn't make too many of these now as his eyes aren't too good. He spent three weeks working only on this one."

"It's very lovely. Thank you," Mona said, putting the necklace back in its box.

"You didn't like it?" the salesman asked. "I can show you another."

"No, it's beautiful. It's just not for me."

"It's very good quality, sister."

"No, thank you," Mona said.

"I'm still hot," Salamat Ali said, pulling the lapels of his shirt collar and fanning himself. Mona also saw a pair of gold bracelets with lion-head finials, like her mother's, the one she had given to Tanya on her marriage. Earlier, she had given away six gold bangles to Amber. She was now left with only two heirlooms: a nose ring and a pair of small earrings. Neither Tanya nor Amber had pierced their noses, so the nose ring was of no use to them. They had also refused to accept her earrings, insisting that she must keep something of her mother's for herself.

The salesman asked Mona if she wanted to try on the bracelets.

"No, I'm just looking today. I'll let you know if I wish to try it on," she said.

The salesman sulkily retired to a corner of the shop and poured himself some tea.

Mona had moved to the far end of the shop to admire a pearl necklace when she caught sight of Salamat Ali's reflection in the mirror. He had his back to her and was talking softly to the salesman. Mona saw the salesman hand him something. Her heart raced for only a moment, then she realized that the *nau-ratan* set was still in the showcase. She was not sure if Salamat Ali had bought something because she did not see him pay the salesman.

"Let's go!" Salamat Ali said, coming towards her.

At the sari shop, Salamat Ali shook his head disapprovingly when Mona showed him the two modestly priced saris she had chosen for his broker's daughter.

"I wish it to be a nice gift," he said. "This won't do."

Mona then chose two saris with *kamdani* work and a Kashmiri shawl. She also bought a few yards of matching silk cloth for petticoats.

"Buy something for yourself, too," Salamat Ali said, before turning to tell the salesman to put everything in a gift bag.

Mona felt stung by his casual tone. It irritated Mona that he casually asked her to choose something for herself while lavishing so much attention on shopping for the broker's daughter.

"How do you like this one?" Salamat Ali asked her after a moment, showing her a light pink cotton dress that came with a light green dupatta. "It's getting warm now. You need something light."

Mona did not like the colours.

"How about this one, then?" Salamat Ali held another dress against her and pointed at the shop mirror.

"I don't like the material," Mona said sharply. "Let's go and eat now. It's too hot."

"As you wish," Salamat Ali said.

Over lunch, Salamat Ali began telling Mona about the broker and the many favours he had done Salamat Ali when he was setting up his business. Mona could not stop thinking about the packet the jewellery salesman had given him.

On the way home the interior of the car felt like an oven. Salamat Ali dropped Mona off, then returned to his office. Mona felt the onset of a headache from being out in the sun too long.

MONA VISITED MRS. BAIG in the evening and returned shortly after Salamat Ali came home. She found him in the kitchen. He had bought some cupcakes and made the tea. The small packet from the jewellery shop lay on the dining table. Salamat Ali pointed to it with a smile.

"What's in it?" she asked.

"See for yourself," he said, pouring the tea.

Mona found a blue velvet box inside. It contained a shining gold nose ring and a pair of earrings. It took Mona a moment to realize that it was her own jewellery. It shone like new because it had been newly polished. She looked up at him.

"When did you take them for polishing?" she asked.

Salamat Ali smiled. "Three days ago."

"I never saw you take them," Mona said. Despite the slight unease she felt at the idea of Salamat Ali going through her jewellery box without telling her, she did not say anything. She was touched by his gesture.

"Come, let's have tea now," Salamat Ali said, opening

the packet of cupcakes. "I bought these specially for you from your favourite bakery."

Later that evening, when Mona opened her wardrobe to put away the nose ring and the earrings, she found the saris and shawls from the shop hanging in the cupboard. Mona quickly turned around. Salamat Ali was standing near the dresser with a smile on his face. He held the *nau-ratan* necklace in his hands, and beckoned to her as he opened the clasp. The bracelets with lion-head finials lay on the dresser.

MONA TOOK OUT THE *nau-ratan* set again a few days later to admire it. When Noori came out of the bathroom after cleaning it, she saw the jewellery lying on the bed.

"Mona bibi, is it yours? It's so beautiful."

Despite a clear disparity in their ages and circumstances, Mona could not disguise her pride as she showed off Salamat Ali's gift.

Seeing that Noori was unable to take her eyes off it, Mona began to feel sorry for her. "Do you want to try it on?" she asked.

"No bibi, no!" Noori stepped back.

"Don't be shy. Try it on in the mirror," Mona said. "I'm asking you to."

"Really, Mona bibi?" Noori said, glancing at her and then at the set.

Salamat Ali came in while Noori stood before the mirror adorned in the *nau-ratan* set.

"What are you doing with that?" he asked her rudely, ignoring Mona.

Mona saw that he was clearly annoyed. "It's okay, Salamat," she said. "She was looking at it, and I asked her to try it on for a moment."

"That's enough," he said to the girl. "Take it off and go back to your work!" Without another word, he turned and left the room.

When Mona tried to comfort Noori, she was surprised to find that the girl was not offended by the rebuke. If anything, Noori tried to convince Mona that she was in the wrong, that she should not have tried on the necklace, regardless of what Mona said. This made Mona feel even sorrier for her. Noori took it off and carefully put it back in the box. She left the room with lowered head.

Mona did not say anything to Salamat Ali about the incident. She realized that he had felt insulted, seeing a servant wearing the gift he had bought her.

A week later, when dressing for a party, Mona opened her jewellery drawer and found the *nau-ratan* set and the bracelets missing.

Mona remembered that Sajid Mir often admonished her about being careless with money, because she sometimes left coins and small bills lying around in view of the servants. *Don't test the honesty of poor people,* he would say. *Don't put temptation in their way. You can't blame them afterwards. It's you who will have corrupted them.*

MONA WAS UNABLE to persuade Noori to return the jewellery. She used every method of persuasion, telling her that they would not dismiss her if she confessed and returned it, then offering a thousand rupees in cash, and in the end even reminding her of the silver nose ring they had given her. Noori remained adamant that she had never touched the jewellery after the day Mona let her try it on. She pretended that she had not seen the bracelets at all. Hard as Mona found it to accept that her trusted maid could be a thief, she knew that Noori must be lying: the bracelets had been in plain view near the *nau-ratan* set.

Finally Salamat Ali asked Mona to let him talk to the girl. While he was closeted in the drawing room with Noori, Mona caught Habib eavesdropping on them and sent him back to the kitchen.

An hour later, Noori emerged from the drawing room, followed by Salamat Ali. She was in tears and went straight to the kitchen.

"She's very thick-skinned," Salamat Ali told Mona. "I'm leaving the matter in your hands now. If you want to report the matter to the police—and I think we should—I'll call them when I return this evening. I've got to go back to the office now for a few hours. Today I couldn't get any work done. A total waste of time."

After he left, Mona went into the kitchen, where she found a tear-stained Noori whispering to Habib. He moved away when he saw Mona enter.

"Salamat Ali wants to report the matter to the police, and I'm also thinking about it. Do you know what they'll do to you?" Mona said.

Noori started sobbing loudly.

"You have two days to come clean," Mona told her, and left the room.

In the end, Mona could not bring herself to report the matter to the police. Noori had an unhappy marriage, was only nineteen, and had three children. At the same time, Mona could not employ someone who was a thief. On the third day she dismissed her from service and asked Amber to look for someone trustworthy to replace her.

When Noori did not come to pick up her salary for the days she had already worked that month, Mona sent Habib to deliver the maidservant's money.

NEXT, MONA BEGAN to worry about Salamat Ali. He started coming home later and later, and when he did he was often drunk. His mood fluctuated on those days. Mona did not know how to cope with his drunken state. Afraid he might fall or injure himself, she lay awake nights until he fell asleep. Finally, Mona could not take it any longer. She asked him one morning if something was bothering him.

"It's just anxiety about my business deal," he said. "I want to make sure everything goes smoothly."

"Don't worry, it'll all be well," Mona replied. "Don't you have the advance?"

"I did, but it was not much and they paid it to keep me from signing some kind of deal with their competitors. Nothing was signed by them."

Mona knew something had gone wrong with the contract when a few days later Salamat Ali came home and told her that the company was renegotiating to change certain parts of the contract.

"I'm not sure any more," he said. "If it falls through, all the work I've done so far will have been for nothing."

Mona thought it careless of Salamat Ali not to have signed papers to protect himself, but she did not say anything. She did not wish to be seen as prying into his business affairs. A few times she had thought of asking him about his business but hadn't, fearing unpleasantness similar to her discussions with Akbar Ahmad. Early in her first marriage, she had noticed Akbar Ahmad's agitation even if she made any casual inquiries during the preparation of the federal budget. He became very secretive, and once he even cross-questioned Mona as if he suspected her of fishing for information. At first Mona had found his manner ridiculous, and just to irritate him she had insisted on finding out more. She finally stopped when his accusatory manner became unbearable. Mona was content to leave Salamat Ali's business matters alone, because unlike with Akbar Ahmad, she felt that with all the attention he lavished on her, she was sufficiently involved in his life.

THE FOLLOWING NIGHT Mona came downstairs and found Salamat Ali putting some papers into an envelope. It was late and she had not heard him come in.

"You're still awake?" he asked.

Mona thought he sounded annoyed.

"I couldn't sleep," Mona said. "When did you come in? What are these papers?"

"The car," he said. "It badly needs repairs. I was looking for the warranty and insurance papers."

"Repairs? Now?" Mona was surprised. "Would you find a garage open at this hour?"

"One in Sher Shah Colony might be open. I'll leave it there overnight and pick it up after work tomorrow."

Mona watched with concern as he returned to sorting through papers.

"What if the car breaks down on the way? Wouldn't it be dangerous to drive at this hour of the night?"

He looked up quickly. "Nothing will happen. I'll be able to get it there without a problem. If there're any minor problems on the way, I can fix them myself."

"Then I'll come with you," Mona said.

"No, Mona." His tone was gentle but firm. "Go to sleep. I'll be back soon."

Mona finally relented, though she remained worried.

After a few days, she noticed that in the mornings, Salamat Ali looked relaxed again. "Maybe the contract is being finalized after all," she thought.

When she came down for breakfast one day, Salamat Ali was already up and eating. He told her that the estimate the mechanic had given for the car was almost equal to the price he had paid for it. Rather than have it repaired, he had asked the mechanic to sell it for him.

"I'll buy us a new one, as soon as this one is sold," he told her as he spread marmalade on his toast. "Old cars are a pain anyway."

WHEN SALAMAT ALI came home for lunch a week later, Mona could see he was troubled again.

After serving him in silence, she finally asked, "Anything the matter?"

"The broker called," Salamat Ali said without looking up.

"And?"

"The contract has been put on hold indefinitely. The company we're dealing with had to shut down two of their plants because of safety issues. At least this is what they're telling us."

"Don't worry. They'll open. Hopefully soon."

"That is not all."

Mona braced herself for some bad news.

"The company bosses have said that they'll put the renewal clause in the contract only if I return a part of the advance money I'd been paid for setting up their distribution channel. They want a more limited operation now."

"That's unfair. First they refused to sign any documents and now this. But is that all?" Mona felt relieved that the news was not quite as bad as she had expected.

"Yes, that's all. But it means everything to my business."

"You can always refuse to pay, and find another company to deal with."

"I can't. I'd already made long-term distribution plans."

"Do you need any money to return the advance?"

"No," Salamat Ali said. "If the car sells in time, I'd be able to manage. I hope it sells soon."

His words took Mona by surprise. She had worried about his business, which now seemed in constant jeopardy, but had not known that Salamat Ali's financial state was so precarious that he would depend on the sale of the old car to pay back the advance.

Mona decided to get more involved in his business, if only to support him in any further difficult situations. She realized only now how generous he had been to buy her all that expensive gold jewellery. She suddenly felt angry again at Noori. If she had reported the matter to the police, surely they would have recovered the gold from her maidservant.

Two days later, Salamat Ali told Mona that the car had been sold. He made the required payment to the company.

MONA VISITED the car dealership and looked at some models. She admired a silver sedan. The salesman offered her the car for a test drive, but not wishing to disclose her inability to drive, Mona made an excuse and left. After arriving home she called Hina. She had already discussed her decision with her sister and had asked Jafar for information about what to look for in a car. Hina told Mona that she would accompany her to test-drive the car and help her make the purchase when she was ready. Jafar would drop them at the dealership.

Several times that day, Mona looked at the glossy brochure she had picked up from the dealership. It showed the same silver model she had chosen. She could not understand most of the specifications listed in the brochure, but read them over and over again with satisfaction. When she heard Salamat Ali come in, she hid the brochure.

"YOU SHOULD ALSO PAY some attention to Salamat Ali's appearance," Hina said to Mona as they were driving back to her house from the car dealership. "It would look bad for all of us if Salamat Ali keeps appearing in his outdated costumes at family gatherings." She quickly added, "In the beginning, Jafar was no better in the matters of wardrobe. If it weren't for me, he'd have kept wearing his old shirts until they fell off his back."

Hina had work to do at home and could not stay for lunch, so Mona sent Habib to get a taxi for her. Before her sister left, Mona asked her to park the car in the shaded area of the driveway. Once she was alone, Mona first draped the car with a sheet, then, for greater effect, decided to leave it uncovered. She asked Bano, the new maidservant she had hired at Amber's recommendation, to wash the driveway, and Mona followed her around to make sure she did not splash water on the car or scratch it accidentally with the broom handle.

Mona kept an eye on the gate from the kitchen door. When she saw Salamat Ali arrive, she went out.

"What's all this?" he asked, staring at the car in the driveway, his expression bemused and incredulous.

With an almost childish joy she dangled the car keys before him. "It's my turn to surprise you."

"But this is a new car?"

"Yes, it is!"

"You spent all of this—!" Salamat Ali began, but Mona put her hand on his mouth.

"Not a word now!" she said.

Seeing his face brighten, Mona felt excited. Though the car had been a considerable expense, she could afford it. It still did not compare with Salamat Ali's generous gift of the jewellery, she thought. Seeing how happy the car made him, she felt she could not be more pleased if Salamat Ali had spent all that money on her.

"When are we going for a ride?" he asked her.

"This evening," she answered. "And I've already decided where."

After dinner, Mona gave directions and Salamat Ali drove them to the tailor shop Jafar had recommended. There Mona asked the elderly tailor to take her husband's measurements for a suit. Salamat Ali stopped him and pulled Mona aside.

"What is wrong?" Mona asked.

"First you bought the car, Mona. And now tailored clothes? This is too much. If it makes you happy to see me in a tailored suit, I'll get it made. But not now. There are problems. With the business, I mean. It wouldn't be right for me to spend the money on a suit when I should be trying to put together some cash for the business."

"It is your money, too. It's ours," Mona said. "You never talk to me about your business. What is it that you need? What is happening?"

"I'll tell you on the way home." Salamat Ali said.

"At least let the tailor take your measurements."

"Not today."

Promising the tailor that they would return soon, Mona walked out with Salamat Ali.

"So what was all that about?" she said when they were in the car. "Why don't you tell me about your business problems?"

"Mona, listen. It would be wrong of me to make any assumptions. If I were supporting us it would be a different matter. You're financially independent. Remember, we had that agreement. Your letter. You liked it that way, you said, and of course I respected that."

Mona realized that Salamat Ali had misunderstood her meaning when she wrote about her financial independence. She felt remorse over hurting his pride, but decided that rather than offer any explanations she should let her actions speak for themselves.

Some days later Mona withdrew three hundred thousand rupees from her bank and gave it to Salamat Ali to put into his business.

"While you focus on getting contracts, you should not have to worry about paying your office expenses," she told him. "Keep this amount as a reserve and let me know when it runs out."

"I don't know what to say, Mona." Salamat Ali looked overwhelmed. "This is too much."

"Your happiness is more important to me than any money in the world," Mona said.

Years ago, she had longed to hear these words herself. Her eyes welled up with tears.

"I would not accept it ordinarily, but I am in a very tight spot these days. I will consider this a loan, Mona. It will be a huge relief, let me tell you. I will be able to breathe easy again. In fact, let us treat this as your investment in my business. At ten per cent profit per year."

"If that is what makes you comfortable, let it be my investment." She was only happy that he had accepted the money.

"It would make me feel so much better," he said, wiping her tears and kissing her.

As they stood embracing, Mona decided to bring up the visit to the tailor shop. "And you must look like a proper businessman," she said, pulling back and gazing up at him. "You need some new suits, too."

"Ah, I knew that was coming," said Salamat Ali. "I knew there was a catch."

"Now will you listen to your investors or not?" Mona asked with mock anger.

"As if I have a choice!" Salamat Ali gave in readily. "Now I have put both my life and business in your hands."

"And it's the best decision you could have made," Mona said, combing his hair with her fingers.

The next day, Salamat Ali accompanied her to the tailor shop, where Mona ordered two summer suits for Salamat Ali and one for the winter.

"Should I go ahead?" The tailor looked hard at Salamat Ali.

"Of course," Salamat Ali said with a smile.

"Only if you're sure," the old man said tonelessly. He picked up his tape and started measuring the length of the sleeves.

On the way home Mona and Salamat Ali bought shoes, socks and several ties.

VIII

THE TRANSfORMATION

The shop where Mona often bought her clothes was on Tariq Road. As it was a short distance from her house, she walked there to pick up a blouse she was having altered. On the way, she passed a group of men standing in the queue outside the bank. She felt their eyes on her body. She kept walking but she stepped a little unsteadily and her mind was unfocused. She would have passed right by the shop if the salesman had not greeted her.

On the way back, Mona went into a bookshop. She caught herself staring at a man who was buying a magazine from a newspaper stall outside, and realized she was ogling someone as young as Faraz and Kamal. A moment later, when he entered the shop, his eyes met hers. Unconsciously, Mona held his gaze for a moment too long. As she saw him come towards her, Mona felt her breathing become irregular. She lowered her eyes from confusion and embarrassment.

He was standing opposite her.

Mona could hardly breathe.

"Excuse me, do I know you?" he asked in a polite voice.

"No!" Mona's face had turned red.

"I thought you were—"

"Excuse me, please!" Mona snatched a book from the shelf without looking at the title and walked briskly to the cashier. She hurried out without counting the change.

After a year of marriage to Salamat Ali, Mona's awakening desire still embarrassed her, but it was a source of pleasure that she found increasingly difficult to resist. Her relationship with Salamat Ali had stirred in her a dormant sense of sensuality. At first, she was disgusted by his habit of walking around naked in the bedroom and shocked at his pulling the sheets off and turning on the lights while she lay undressed in bed. Akbar Ahmad had always had a sheet covering them during sex. There was no question of lights: Akbar Ahmad even kept on his shirt and socks. The pyjamas, too, were only lowered to the knees.

Though Mona had been drunk at the beach house, a guilty pleasure had overwhelmed her as she abandoned herself to her desire for the first time. Slowly, however, Mona began reciprocating Salamat Ali's interest in her body unreservedly. She desired his touch. She always felt guilty and ashamed afterwards, but that did not prevent it from happening again. She now spent a lot of time every morning critically inspecting her body in the mirror and taking greater care of herself, using age-defying creams for her skin although there were no wrinkles on her face. Her body, similarly, showed no visible marks of aging.

What had transformed and revitalized her existence also at times made Mona feel insecure. She feared Salamat Ali's interest might wane. She had discovered that while he took an interest in her body, there were no finer, gentler feelings that guided his interest. While Salamat Ali was a very different person from Akbar Ahmad, she could not expect any more emotional tenderness from him than she had received from her first husband. It had taken her a long time to admit this to herself. What had taken her even longer to acknowledge, however, was that comments and praise that would have sounded to her as almost superficial before she met Salamat Ali, could satisfy her and make her happy. She felt pleased enough each time Salamat Ali complimented her on her appearance, or when she put on a new dress for him. He was never at a loss for compliments even if he made them in his own unrefined manner.

When she came home, Mona went upstairs to try on the clothes. She was unbuttoning her blouse in the mirror when she saw Salamat Ali approach from the side. He was home for lunch. She saw that he wanted to surprise her. A smile spread on her face. When he had just reached behind her, Mona slowly turned around and kissed him hard on the mouth.

Salamat Ali whispered in her ear. "You look so beautiful."

That day his words brought tears to her eyes as she was overwhelmed by the sense of loss she felt in the cruel fate that had joined her to Akbar Ahmad in marriage.

"What did I say, Mona?" Salamat Ali stared at her with a confused look. "I just said you looked beautiful. What is wrong with that?"

"And old!" she retorted.

"Who said that? You look more beautiful than all these twenty-year-olds walking up and down the streets!"

"But I looked better before!" she said, and began sobbing. "I looked more beautiful when I was younger!"

Salamat Ali continued to stare uncomprehendingly.

She again kissed him hard on the mouth.

"You almost tore off my lips!" Salamat Ali laughed. "Not that I'm complaining."

"Then shut up!" Mona said. She looked at him with the intensity of desire. Her hands slid over his face, neck and his arms. She caressed his body. A devilish smile appeared on his face. He pulled her towards him and pushed her onto the bed. Her hands stroked his body even as he quickly undressed her. Her unblinking eyes were transfixed on him.

Physical desire came into full bloom inside Mona. What she had felt in her adolescence was a vague shadow of the sensation she now felt. The misguided sense of virtue, piety, and modesty she had exercised in her intimate moments with Salamat Ali on their first night together, when distracted by thoughts of her widowhood, was now dispelled.

An hour later, they were still in bed when Mona heard someone coming up the stairs. She had not realized that the bedroom door had been left open.

"Mona! Are you there?" Mrs. Baig called from the staircase. From long habit, she had walked into the house without knocking.

Salamat Ali was lying near the edge of the bed and nearly fell off as Mona rushed to close the door, pulling a sheet to cover herself. In her confusion she had kept holding on to the pillow as well.

"Was that you, Mona?" Mrs. Baig asked as the door suddenly closed on her face with a bang. "Oh, I'm sorry!"

Salamat Ali's body was convulsing with laughter, which he muffled by covering his face with the sheets. Mona threw the pillow at him.

SALAMAT ALI'S TRANSFORMATION was all too conspicuous when he wore his new suit to Hina and Jafar's wedding anniversary a few weeks later. Although his new clothes fit him well, he seemed ill at ease. But everyone noticed the happy look on Mona's face. Her peals of laughter held no ring of artificiality or falsehood. She looked stunning in her new *kamdani* sari.

"I can't believe it's Mummy," Amber told Hina.

Hina looked at her sister for a moment. "I do. I knew the same Mona once."

"When?" Amber asked.

"Long ago, before . . ." Hina walked away leaving the sentence unfinished.

Umar Shafi was there, too, sitting with a plate loaded with cookies and pastries and watching everything from a corner. Hina had told Mona that Rubab and Umar Shafi were now officially engaged and the wedding invitations were being printed.

"A match made in heaven?" Mona had commented.

Umar Shafi greeted neither Mona nor Salamat Ali. Mona herself was keen to avoid any contact with him.

"A few days ago, I saw Umar Shafi near my office," Salamat Ali told Mona. "He pretended not to see me."

"He did you a favour," Mona said. "He's insufferable."

Jafar's cousin Imad walked over to them and said, "How are you, Mona? You haven't introduced me to your husband yet."

"Oh, I thought I did." She suddenly felt embarrassed introducing Salamat Ali to him. "This is Jafar's cousin, Imad. And this is . . . Salamat Ali." Mona still had difficulty using the word "husband" when introducing Salamat Ali. She felt she must be conceited like Hina or ashamed of Salamat Ali's social standing, and she felt guilty for her inability to overcome these feelings. But at the same time, she was aware that there was something about Salamat Ali's personality, and his image in her eyes, that did not allow her to relate to him as her husband.

Salamat Ali nudged Imad. "I think I see gulab jamans on the table."

"Why don't you go ahead. I'll only have this cup of black tea," Imad said, pointing to his cup.

"Watching your tummy, eh?" Salamat Ali said, poking Imad in the stomach.

"Well, yes, I guess you can say that. If I don't, I'll get one." Imad smiled.

"So you have an office in Karachi now," Mona said quickly, trying to divert attention from Salamat Ali's embarrassing act while he made his way to the table, whistling to himself.

"Yes, I do. I thought there was a good opportunity for us."

"Is your office fully functional now?" Mona asked.

"Yes, it is. If you wish . . ." He left the sentence incomplete.

Mona thought Imad had meant to invite her to see the office. She also sensed that he had, unconsciously perhaps, moved a little closer.

Nervously she changed the subject. "Are we going to see many fancy landmark buildings in the city?"

"Not really. We work mainly in the low-cost housing sector. But I do read a lot about the monumental architecture. I really don't like modernistic buildings. I should clarify: they leave me cold. The execution, not the philosophy."

"I don't know much about monuments, but I do admire our classical architecture," Mona said.

"I do, too. They had a modernistic philosophy as well, but they knew that a basic human aesthetic has to be followed to blend a building with the people. They played with watercourses, with the flora. Some of the floral panels they use are really faux windows looking into an imaginary garden."

"That's such a beautiful thought," Mona said. "When I see them next it'll be with a new appreciation."

"And then there's the Taj Mahal," Imad continued. "You could never get an idea of its beauty from just photographs. One has to see it to realize its grandeur."

"Discussing the Taj Mahal, are we?" Salamat Ali had quietly walked between them with his plate of gulab jamans. "Love is in the air, yes?"

Mona saw that his rude intrusion had irritated Imad. She felt uncomfortable herself.

"Mona and I are planning to go see the Taj Mahal on our honeymoon." Salamat Ali put his arm around her waist and pulled her towards him.

"That's very nice. I hope you'll enjoy your visit," Imad said.

Mona looked incredulously at Salamat Ali. He had never discussed any of it with her. She also felt that it was bizarre to mention a honeymoon now, after they had been married a year. And if he was lying, it was a silly thing to lie about.

"Tell me, Imad," Salamat Ali said. "Didn't the emperor kill the architect who designed the Taj Mahal? Now, why do you think that was so? To keep him from designing other such buildings, or was there something else?" He nudged Imad and winked.

"I am not too sure the story is true," Imad said.

"Really?" Salamat Ali said, glancing at Mona. "And why's that?"

"Architects, I mean good architects," Imad said, looking Salamat Ali in the eye, "aren't stupid. They know a despot when they see one. I am sure they know how to keep a safe distance."

Salamat Ali laughed nervously.

"Now, if you'll excuse me, I think Jafar is looking for me," Imad said, and left without looking at Mona.

"You never told me about any visit to see the Taj Mahal," Mona said as Imad walked away.

"Oh, I had meant it as a surprise for you, but then I got too tied up at work," he said dismissively, still staring after Imad.

"It was sweet of you to think of it," Mona said. "But why didn't you ever tell me?"

Salamat Ali was quiet.

"You two seemed to be having a good time," he said after a moment. "I saw how you were chirping away with him."

"I only spoke to him briefly." Mona felt shocked and embarrassed. She also felt a little guilty.

Salamat Ali stared at her as he ate his gulab jaman.

Hina later took Mona aside. "Is it true that you withdrew another three hundred thousand from the bank after buying the car?" she asked.

"Yes," Mona answered casually. "It was for Salamat Ali's business. Why? How did you find out?"

"The accountant came yesterday to have Jafar look over your tax papers. He mentioned that in passing." After Akbar Ahmad's death, Jafar's accountant looked after the accounts set up for Mona and her daughters.

Mona did not say anything further to Hina, but she did not like her tone and her manner of inquiring about the transaction. Mona decided to have a word with the accountant.

On the drive home, she began to feel angry with her whole family. She thought she had detected a condescending attitude in Imad's manner as he talked to Salamat Ali. Imad seemed to be making fun of him. Why should anyone make fun of Salamat Ali? What gave him the right? If Imad wished to invite her to see his office, he must also invite Salamat Ali.

When they reached home it was still too early for their bedtime. Mona wanted some fresh air, so she took a stroll in the garden while Salamat Ali went upstairs to change.

When she came up a little later, he looked at her strangely. She did not pay attention to it, and went into the bathroom.

"Why did Hina take you aside at the party?" Salamat Ali asked, as she removed her makeup.

"Oh, that! She was telling me something about her son and daughter-in-law," Mona lied. "Just some family gossip."

She had been irritated earlier when Salamat Ali interrupted her conversation with Imad. Now that feeling returned.

A WEEK LATER, Salamat Ali bought Mona half a dozen saris and several new dresses. It overwhelmed her, since her wardrobe had been limited to a few old saris and two or three dresses. They lasted her long because she took care of them. Mona decided to replace her old clothes now.

As Mona made a pile of clothes to pass on, she wondered whether Salamat Ali's financial woes may have been the result of his reckless spending habits. She could only guess that he had bought the clothes for her from the money she had given him for day-to-day business expenses. Not that his gesture displeased her. At first, she had laughed at the bright colours. But when she tried the garments on, she realized that Salamat Ali had a good eye for colours that complimented her.

Tanya and Amber came over for lunch, and while they ate, Mona told them about the clothes. Later, she took them to the bedroom to show them her new wardrobe. When they came down, Mona brought the old clothes with her to the living room. She picked the dress she had decided to give to Mrs. Baig's maidservant and left Amber and Tanya to take it across the street.

Mrs. Baig was out, so Mona returned almost immediately. She overheard Tanya from the corridor, and her daughter's resentful tone brought Mona to a standstill a few steps from the door. "Some of them are like new," Tanya was saying as she rummaged through the clothes, picking them up and dropping them back in the heap. "She never used to discard them in this condition before."

"Can't you see they're too old-fashioned?" Amber answered. "And they *are* old. I'm not surprised she's getting rid of them."

"No, there's been a change in her. Can't you see? First it was the car. What do they need a sedan for? A mini would have been enough for the two of them. You know, when I was getting married, Mrs. Kazi told Mummy that their family didn't need any dowry—she only wanted a car so that it would become a little easier for Faraz to search for a job. Daddy said they couldn't afford it. It was not all that long ago either. And at the time he was getting a salary. How could she afford to buy a car now? I see her wearing new clothes whenever I come here or see her at someone else's house. Now he, too, has started dressing up. How ridiculous he looked all dressed up at Aunt Hina's party." Mona restrained her urge to enter the room and confront Tanya. She told herself that it was her own fault. If she had talked to Tanya herself about her decision to remarry rather than communicating it through Hina, perhaps much of the resentment her daughter felt could have been avoided.

"Don't say anything of this to Mummy," Amber said. "The car was necessary for her. It's not safe for her to go around in taxis. I'm glad she finally bought one. Kamal was irritated when she asked to be dropped somewhere. I remember you telling me that Faraz also doesn't like to drive people around. And as for the clothes and the jewellery—maybe he's buying them. How would you know? In all the time that she was married she didn't even buy a single gold set for herself, while Aunt Hina had seven. I'm sure it's his money."

"It's not his. I checked at the bank." Tanya had lowered her voice a little.

"You mean the car?"

"No! There was another withdrawal too."

"What other withdrawal?"

"Another three hundred thousand was drawn a little later. I wanted to ask her last night, but Salamat Ali hardly ever left her alone. I didn't want to call you last night because Mrs. Kazi would have heard of it. And when I phoned you from work today you had already left to come here."

"Three hundred thousand," Amber slowly repeated to herself.

"Mummy was the principal heir but you and I both have our own share. Faraz was telling me last night that it would've been improper to ask for the estate's division immediately after Daddy's death, but now that she's made her own home—"

"Stop it! She'll be returning any minute," Amber said.

"No, please don't stop," Mona said as she entered the room, unable to bear it any longer. "It's better that she speaks her mind freely today. Let all her venom come out." She turned to Tanya. "I'll call Jafar and have the estate papers drawn out and notarized as you desire. You can take them to your husband and tell him not to show his face around here again."

"Faraz didn't say anything," Tanya said quickly.

"Mummy, nobody said anything—" Amber said.

"I don't care what that bloody Faraz said or didn't say. All I needed to hear I heard from her own mouth." Mona shot a fiery glance at Tanya. "You resent it that your mother—after spending her life for you and your father—has some left for herself? You resent it when someone finally pays me a little attention and I'm happy? You've inherited the same selfish streak your father had. All my married life I suffered because of it. But now I won't take it any more. Both of you will get your share according to the law. After that, don't you ever open your mouth about my life and what I do with it. Who gave you the right to ask what I do with the money? I could see the look on Faraz's face when he saw Salamat Ali at Hina's party. Your husband shouldn't forget that Salamat Ali is a self-made man, while Faraz was dependent on my handouts until recently. Where did you think that money came from, the money I gave you for household expenses when he was not working? That was what I had kept of my own savings. Your father never knew about it. I didn't tell him because if he had learned about it, he'd have stopped me from giving it and said something insulting to Faraz besides. Only Hina knew how I had saved up that money over ten years, denying myself every small comfort and sometimes even basic necessities. Did your father ever tell me he had the money? No! Once when I gave him a hint about your circumstances, he became furious and said we barely had enough for our own expenses. Can you guess how I felt after learning that the money was always there? About being deceived in that manner? I've hidden all this from both of you until now, but no more. Your father put me through this misery for what? If I had died first, I'd never have known. After thirty years of deception and betrayal, I'm sure he'd have been able to continue living with himself. Now you come along—"

"Mummy—" Tanya said.

"Shut up!" Mona said. "All that came out of his mouth whenever I asked to be allowed some small expense was 'No! We must save! We must save!' An outing, a picnic, a dinner alone somewhere was too much to ask. If I spend any money now on myself or Salamat Ali, it's the money your father saved at my expense—or do you think I had no right as a wife to what he earned after I slaved for him from morning till night?"

She could see that both Tanya and Amber were shocked by the outpouring of her anger. They listened in surprise and disbelief. They had never heard her express even the slightest grievance against Akbar Ahmad. But at that moment she did not care how they felt.

"And your dowry," Mona said, looking at Tanya. "I asked Akbar Ahmad several times to find out if we could get a bank loan to buy you the car Mrs. Kazi wanted so badly. I remember well how Faraz sat there shamelessly, without ever once saying he could do without the car. Not even for the sake of appearances. From the way their family carried on, it seemed that Faraz was so perfectly immobile that only a wheelchair could have solved his problems. Again your father said we could not afford it. And that was the end of the matter. Perhaps it was his revenge for your marrying against his wishes—unless it was his miserable inability to spend money on anything except to fill his belly. But I feel very glad now that we didn't buy you the car. Neither you nor your bloody husband deserve it!"

With that, Mona stormed out of the room.

LATER, WHEN SHE WAS LYING in the bedroom, she heard them leave quietly. Mona no longer felt angry, only exhausted. She had never imagined that she could one day unburden herself before her daughters in that manner. Until now, such a disclosure would have been the betrayal of her marriage, and of her status as a mother. It would have seemed almost sacrilegious. But after venting, this no longer mattered to her. She did not feel threatened by what her daughters or anyone else thought of her life. She was still living it.

When the phone rang, Mona instinctively knew who it was. She felt saddened because she had indirectly made Amber, too, the target of her rebukes.

"Amber?" Mona said.

"Mummy!" Amber's voice was hoarse from crying.

Mona stifled a sob.

She sat there holding the receiver to her ear.

"LUNCH IS ALL FINISHED," Salamat Ali said when Hina walked in.

"Thanks, I already had lunch an hour ago. But I wouldn't mind having a cup of tea." Hina pulled out a chair and sat down.

Mona stood and went to the sink. "I'll put some water to boil."

"I've brought a copy of my application for the second phone line," Hina said, taking the paper from her purse. "I was wondering if you could go, Salamat, and check its status tomorrow in the afternoon when the office opens."

"No trouble at all, Hina," he said.

"But—" Mona turned and looked at Salamat Ali. They had planned to have lunch outdoors the following day.

"We can always have lunch afterwards," he said, noticing Mona looking at him.

"Oh, I didn't know you had other plans. No, no!" Hina began to put the paper back in her purse. "You should keep your lunch engagement. I'll ask Jafar to go. He should be able to find some time after his meeting."

"Give it to me, Hina." Salamat Ali stretched his hand out across the table.

"Oh, okay, if you insist," Hina said, looking toward Mona.

But Mona had turned away to make tea.

After Salamat Ali took the paper from Hina, she got up and moved closer to Mona. "Ever since Jafar started his own consultancy, he's always on the phone. It's been almost six months since we filed the application for the new line and nobody has shown up to activate the connection. Digital phone lines were supposed to eliminate such delays."

"You should have talked to the linesman, you know," Salamat Ali put in. "If you'd done so, the new phone line would have been installed within twenty-four hours. But don't forget that the linesman has a family to take care of, too: his wife to take shopping, his children to send to school. A small gift will alleviate his many sufferings."

Hina held up one hand. "I can't handle this business of bribery, if that's what you mean. And I know Jafar wouldn't want to get involved with it either."

"You aren't doing anything illegal. Isn't your application already on file and the fee paid? The paperwork is all done."

"Still, I feel awkward. And Jafar is no good at dealing with the riff-raff."

"It's quite simple really," Salamat Ali said.

"Could you please take care of it, too, Salamat?" Hina asked, then, when she saw Mona turn to stare at her, adding, "Only if you are not busy."

Salamat Ali spoke before Mona could say anything. "Of course, I'll take care of it." When he left to return to work after drinking a glass of water, Mona did not return his goodbye. Then she turned on Hina.

"Why didn't you call to let me know that you were coming?" Mona asked her sister. Salamat Ali had begun spending too much time running errands for Hina and her household. Whenever Jafar was busy, Hina asked Salamat Ali to drive her to appointments. Salamat Ali always happily obliged. In the beginning, Mona had felt that Hina was making an effort to be friendly towards Salamat Ali. Now the situation was beginning to irk her.

"Same problem. Jafar was on the phone till the last minute and then he began hurrying me—" Hina broke off, noticing Mona's face. "Mona, what's wrong?"

"Nothing," Mona said.

"Why are you so quiet?"

"It's nothing."

"Really?"

"Yes!"

"Mona!"

"Before, you used to call him all sorts of names. And now look at you! He's become indispensable to you for everything. Couldn't you ask Jafar to help you sometimes? Or that Imad?" Mona was unable to hold back any longer. "Why does Salamat have to drive you all over town?" She felt her eyes fill with tears.

Hina burst out laughing. "Stop crying, stupid! I didn't know you'd be jealous of his spending a little time around us. My God, all these years and I never saw this side of you. Come here. Dry your eyes now. Are you out of your mind?"

Mona sat motionless. The relief she had felt after voicing her grievances was already being replaced by embarrassment. She could not look Hina in the eye.

"Of course you must be jealous," Hina said, still laughing. "Who would want such a beauty queen as your Salamat Ali out of the sight for too long?"

When Mona finally smiled, Hina hugged her.

Hina teased her about the incident for many days.

WHEN THE FAMILY commemorated Akbar Ahmad's second death anniversary a month later, Amber invited Mona and Tanya to her house for a late breakfast. Mona had spoken to Amber on the phone several times since her outburst but neither had mentioned the incident. Tanya, however, had neither visited nor called Mona.

Mona had not wished to cast aspersions on Akbar Ahmad's character as a father. Nor did she expect an apology from her daughter for how her father had acted. But Mona did expect Tanya's acknowledgment of the way she had suffered in her life with Akbar Ahmad. That Tanya chose to avoid her meant that she was unwilling to concede even that.

Tanya was already at the gathering when Mona arrived. Kamal was leaving for his office. He was already late for work, and in the exchange of greetings and goodbyes as he hurried out, Mona and Tanya successfully avoided addressing each other directly. Mona had thought that Amber might want to patch things up between her mother and sister, but Amber made no such attempt. Mona was almost grateful she didn't, because she would have found it difficult not to confront Tanya again.

Afterwards, the three of them visited the nearby graveyard to offer prayers for Akbar Ahmad's soul. On the way, they stopped at a roadside flower-seller's hut to buy garlands to place on the grave. The graveyard's old caretaker recognized them and brought a water-sprinkler to wash Akbar Ahmad's gravestone. He also lit an incense stick and then, after he was paid, left them alone to pray.

Tanya placed the garlands on the marble slab.

Mona felt no emotion while praying. With guilty awareness she stole glances at Tanya and Amber's faces. Tanya was praying with lowered head, but Amber averted her gaze when her mother caught her eye. All three seemed uncomfortable during their short, awkward visit.

Tanya insisted on taking Mona home and while in the

car attempted conversation, but Mona did not respond. As she was dropping Mona off, Tanya gave her a garland.

"This is for Daddy's portrait," she said.

Mona took it without a word and shut the car door behind her.

When later hanging the garland around Akbar Ahmad's portrait, her hand touched the frame. Akbar Ahmad stared at her, his eyes glowing with hatred. She felt a pressure on her chest. His presence seemed to suffocate her.

Before Salamat Ali arrived in the evening, she removed the garland, taking care not to touch the portrait. She carried the garland into the kitchen, put it inside an opaque plastic bag and threw it into the garbage, regretting the waste of the fresh flowers.

AFTER THE SECOND ANNIVERSARY of his death, Mona felt Akbar Ahmad watching over her every movement, her every breath. She could see the sardonic look on his face when she waited for Salamat Ali at night. Akbar Ahmad looked at Salamat Ali with ill-disguised contempt, and in Salamat Ali's presence often cast bitter, reproachful glances at Mona.

Mona now spent most of her time away from the living room.

DESPITE AKBAR AHMAD'S oppressive presence, Mona was conscious of other, pleasant changes in her life and of sensations experienced for the first time. There was an easy forgetfulness she had never tasted before. She often lost track of the place she kept the house key and missed the due dates for bill payments. When she went shopping, she sometimes left the bags behind. Tanya was offended when Mona forgot to wish her son a happy birthday. For the first time, however, Mona took pleasure in the happy idleness of her mind rather than worrying about it, or thinking it symptomatic of some disease. Mona's quarterly medical reports came back clear. She forgot the days when she had suffered cramps from sitting in one place for a period of time and had felt constant backaches. She felt attractive. She could read it in the eyes of men.

Mona believed her self-contentment was the result of having Salamat Ali in her life. His gestures of devotion continued. If he had any anxieties or frustrations about his business deals, they never found expression in anger or even inattention towards her. From what Salamat Ali told her of his business now, she could only guess that he was still struggling to find new contracts. After the first loan, she lent him smaller amounts on two other occasions. Things seemed to be going well for a time, but the date by which he had agreed to pay back her loan came and passed, and the loan remained unpaid. Yet she no longer cared about that. She did care when he continued to return home drunk every night. It made him forget himself: once he even undressed with the lights on and the bedroom curtains parted.

Still, Mona forgave these irritants every time she was shown a new token of his regard for her. At first, Salamat Ali merely asked her not to spend so much time in the kitchen. Then Mona noticed that whenever she went to the kitchen to give directions to Habib, or to give him a hand in the food preparation, he became uneasy. Finally, Habib told Mona that he would lose his job if Salamat Ali found out that he had let her do any kitchen work.

Mona was displeased that Salamat Ali had threatened Habib in this manner and she confronted him.

Salamat Ali confessed, saying, "I'd never want these delicate hands smelling of spices. I wouldn't ever want this lovely brow covered with perspiration. Your beauty must not be wasted in doing kitchen chores!"

Mona's displeasure disappeared immediately.

She noticed, too, that when she stopped interfering in Habib's work, his cooking improved, and with that her appetite. It was almost out of habit that she used to spend most of her day in the kitchen, where continuous exposure to spices and the aroma wafting from the pot would saturate her taste buds even before she sat down to eat. Now, she actually savoured her meals.

For the first time she realized how Akbar Ahmad must have enjoyed his food.

IX

THE DISCLOSURE

Jafar, his business partners and their families were invited to a private song recital organized at the home of one of his clients. Mona and Salamat Ali arrived late and so lost the last parking space near the house. Spotting the invitation in Mona's hand, the host at the gate beckoned, and Salamat Ali told Mona to go inside while he parked the car.

The star of the evening was an elderly female singer. Mona was pleased to see from the program that she was going to sing from a selection of *ghazals* of both classical and modern poets. She hoped the musicians would not override the vocals as she had witnessed at some *ghazal* evenings. The *sarangi* and harmonium were usually orderly, though the *tabla* players often ruined the cadence with their raucous playing. Mona sat behind Tanya and Faraz on the carpet in the fourth row. They were sitting all around a small raised stage set up for the singer and the musicians.

Mona worried about Salamat Ali, until she saw him making his way through the audience just as the recital was beginning. White sheets had been spread over the carpet. The lights were dimming. Salamat Ali was swaying slightly.

"I can't see the singer," he said loudly, slumping next to Mona. "Where is she?"

"Shhh!" Mona said. "You can't see her because they have switched off the lights."

She smelled alcohol on his breath and realized he must have been drinking in the car.

"Aha! What do I see here!" Salamat Ali was holding up Faraz's scotch bottle. "I didn't know we could bring liquor!"

Those known to drink had been asked discreetly to bring their own liquor to the recital. Mona became quiet when Faraz said that Jafar had told him to bring his own. Faraz passed a glass of scotch to Salamat Ali.

"Thank you, Faraz. This is what I call showing respect to your elders."

"Salamat, no more please," Mona said. "You've already had some. You have to drive home."

"I'll be fine," he said as the music began. "Don't you worry. And you should have some, too, if you like. It makes the whole thing so much more enjoyable."

During the first half of the performance, Salamat Ali loudly praised the singer. Some people turned to look at him, and a couple sitting in the front row asked him to keep his voice down. After Tanya put her fingers in her ears, he briefly quietened. Although Mona privately told Faraz not to give Salamat Ali any more liquor, at the beginning of the second half of the recital she saw another full glass of scotch in her husband's hand. She confronted Faraz.

"He was insisting, poking me. What could I do?" Faraz laughed.

Salamat Ali winked at Mona.

Mona noticed Tanya looking across the room. She followed her daughter's gaze and caught a glimpse of Amber's parents-in-law. Mona wondered if they had seen anything. Moments later, she spotted Imad sitting behind them. Mona turned her gaze away lest Imad should think she was looking at him. But she noticed Imad was not looking in her direction.

Just then, the audience cheered at the opening notes of a famous *ghazal*. With eyes shut tight, Salamat Ali began drumming furiously on his thighs. Mona heard Faraz's laughter, which came easily when he started drinking. Then Mona saw Salamat Ali scanning the room. She thought he was looking for the washroom, and directed him to it, though she was not sure he heard her. Salamat Ali got up and slowly made his way through the audience in the opposite direction, towards the platform where the singer and musicians were seated.

In the stage lights, Mona saw a glass of scotch balanced on Salamat Ali's head. The singer stared at him. Every eye in the room was now fixed on Salamat Ali, who stood in the middle of the room flailing his arms, shimmying his hips and trying to shake his chest like a female dancer. Half of his scotch had already spilled, dripping down his back and shoulders. Finally, the glass fell to the carpet.

Mona felt as if someone had drained every drop of blood from her body. Tanya moved away from her and appeared to have stopped breathing. Faraz laughed hysterically. As the final song came to an end, a loud guffaw was heard from a corner of the room. Some people were laughing. Others were too shocked at the spectacle to find it humorous.

SALAMAT ALI AT FIRST refused to leave the room, but when Mona caught his wrist, he quietly allowed her to lead him away. Faraz took over to help Salamat Ali out into the courtyard.

Mona followed them to the doorway where she stopped as she heard Hina's voice. Then she overheard Jafar say, "That's why I did not tell him he could bring booze with him. Now look what an ass he's made of himself. Do you think I—"

"Shhh!" Hina, seeing Mona, had stopped Jafar. "If you don't want to drive them, then I will."

"Let me take both of you home," Hina said to Mona.

"No, thank you very much!" Mona said curtly. "I'll manage." She knew she should not get upset with Hina. Salamat Ali was there as Jafar's guest, and it was Jafar who had been made a laughingstock of her husband before his clients.

"As you wish." Hina also seemed angry, and did not insist.

Mona headed for the courtyard to look for Faraz and ask him to drive them home. She hoped he had not had too much to drink. Few taxis were to be had in that residential neighbourhood, and, anyway, it would be risky to take a taxi with Salamat Ali in that state at that hour.

"Mona."

Hearing Imad's voice behind her, she turned.

"Please bring Salamat Ali with me." Imad was standing there holding his car keys.

"No, thanks, I'll . . ." She searched his face for any sign that he might be enjoying her embarrassment. She saw only concern.

"Please come, Mona. I was going in that direction any-way."

She had no strength to resist.

"If you don't mind, we'll put him in the back seat while you sit in front," Imad said as he opened the back door. "I don't want anyone to notice that he's drunk."

Salamat Ali sprawled himself comfortably in the back seat, humming the tune of the last *ghazal*. As Imad drove, Mona turned her head every now and then to make certain her husband was okay.

She thought of her earlier encounter with Imad. After overcoming her anger at Hina prying into her life, she had felt that she had no reason to be angry with him. She cherished their brief conversation. Whenever she thought about it, she was reminded that Hina had said Imad would be a good match for her.

Salamat Ali suddenly lurched forward to whisper in Mona's ear. "Are you two comfortable?"

He gave Mona a terrible start, and Imad too turned quickly. "Salamat, please sit back!" she snapped.

"Just checking!" Salamat Ali said, wagging his finger. "Remember, Uncle Salamat is watching you!"

Mona saw Imad purse his lips. She was mortified.

"Let us have dinner together somewhere," Salamat Ali blurted out.

When nobody answered, he cursed, fell back into his seat, and snored all the way home.

Imad helped Salamat Ali to the bedroom, then took his leave. Mona came down to see him to the door.

"Thank you, Imad. Thank you so much! And I'm sorry about Salamat. He was too drunk."

"There's no need to apologize," Imad said. "Look, I'm sorry if I caused any unpleasantness between you two the other day. I truly am." Then he turned and walked away.

Mona watched him go.

"*Moaaaaaaaaana!*" Salamat Ali began calling her from upstairs.

She looked towards the bedroom a few times but remained where she was.

After a while she turned and slowly climbed the stairs.

In the bedroom, Salamat Ali was lying sideways on the bed. She thought he must have tried to get up after Imad left him. She stood there looking at him angrily, but did not know what to say. Salamat Ali gestured to her to approach, but she turned without speaking and left the room. As she was going downstairs Mona heard him curse.

She made herself some tea but did not drink it. She felt exhausted. She planned to check on Salamat Ali later that night, but instead fell asleep on the sofa in the living room. In her dream she saw Akbar Ahmad with a knowing smile on his face trying to say something to her.

〰

AMBER CALLED THE NEXT AFTERNOON. Her in-laws had come to their house to relate what they had witnessed. She had not fully believed Tanya's story of the night before. Amber told Mona that Kamal had said nothing, but she now found it hard to face her in-laws.

Mona did not know what to say. When Bano called her from downstairs, she said goodbye to Amber and hung up the phone.

"When do you want me to clean the room?" asked the maidservant. "Salamat Sahib is still sleeping."

"Leave the room for today," she told her. "You can do it tomorrow."

Half an hour later, Mona saw Bano drying the utensils in the kitchen. Once again, she had not washed her hands after handling the mopping rag. Mona sent her to the washroom to wash her hands with soap and put the utensils back into the kitchen sink to be washed again. The girl apparently had no sense of cleanliness, and Mona tired of monitoring her. Habib too complained about her.

Mona missed Noori.

MONA'S EMBARRASSMENT was so great that she did not call Hina for two days. Her distress worsened when she didn't hear from Hina either. Mona was still furious with Salamat Ali, although he had profusely apologized to her the next morning. His drunken antics had invited the kind of public scrutiny Mona found unbearable and had tarnished her respectable image.

On the morning of the third day after the performance, she mustered the courage to call Hina and express her regret over the incident.

Jafar answered the phone. "Let me get Hina for you," he said when he heard Mona's voice.

She was insulted, but felt she could not say anything. Then a troubling thought occurred to her. She hung up the phone without waiting for Hina to answer.

Her sister called a few minutes later, and Mona gave vent to her feelings. "Why am I being treated in this manner? Yes, Salamat was drunk and made a fool of himself, but that doesn't mean that when I call your home Jafar can dispense with the courtesy of a greeting. I won't put up with any expectations that Salamat Ali should have a higher standard of conduct than other men in our family."

"Mona, calm down!" Hina said.

"No, I won't calm down. I didn't approve of what Salamat did, and I'll apologize to both you and Jafar over and over again about it, but I get the feeling that neither you nor Jafar ever truly accepted Salamat Ali into the family. If Faraz had done something of this nature, I wouldn't have ostracized Tanya. Would Jafar have acted the same way if your own son had done it?" Mona felt even angrier that she did not have the face to confront Jafar about not telling Salamat Ali to bring his own liquor.

"Mona, please listen to me!"

"I'm listening."

"Jafar was upset about the incident, of course, but he had gotten over it by the next day. He also called his client earlier today. There was no unpleasantness."

"So everything is okay?" Mona paused. "Then why—?"

At that moment she heard Salamat Ali calling her from upstairs.

"We need to talk. Is he home?" Hina asked.

"Who, Salamat? What do you mean? Why do you ask?"

"I can't discuss this over the phone, Mona. But we must talk. Urgently! Jafar's heard something upsetting. He called his lawyer for a consultation this morning. We were discussing the situation with him in his study when you called. That was why Jafar rushed back."

"What is it all about? What is going on? Why are you being so mysterious and what has the lawyer got to do with it?"

"Mona, don't worry, everything will be okay. Right now I need to talk to you in person, and alone. Can you come here in a taxi? Or can you meet me somewhere else?"

"I'll come over."

Mona went upstairs to see Salamat Ali. It was half past ten and he was still asleep, suffering from a bad hangover from another night of drinking. He had taken a vacation that day to drive to Hyderabad in the afternoon with Mona. Hina's mysterious tone had filled Mona with foreboding, but when she laid eyes on Salamat Ali, she felt the same affectionate compassion for him that she had always felt.

Downstairs again, she gave instructions to Habib to get a taxi for her and then to prepare Salamat Ali's breakfast. She told Bano that she was going to her sister's house and that she should tell Salamat Ali, when he came down, that she would be back in an hour or two.

~~~

"WHAT ARE YOU DOING TODAY?" Hina asked as Mona walked in. Jafar stood nearby with a file in his hand. "Salamat Ali is taking me to Hyderabad to shop for bangles. What did you want to tell me, Hina?"

"Jafar will explain."

"What's going on?" Mona turned to Jafar, who pulled up a chair and sat down opposite her.

"Let me give you a little background, Mona," Jafar said, "about what you're going to hear." Hina stood by the side-board, her expression unreadable.

"I wish there were an easier way of telling you this, but there isn't," Jafar said. "The sooner you know, the better it will be for you and everyone concerned."

Mona froze with foreboding. A sense of helplessness overtook her.

"We discovered and verified that Salamat Ali doesn't have a registered business. He does have an office, but the business itself doesn't exist. There are no tax filings, no records of any kind. In other words, it's all a hoax."

"That's ridiculous," Mona said. "There are hundreds of unregistered businesses in the city that operate under the owner's name. That means nothing." The news had restored her confidence. If it was only a matter of business regulation, she need not worry.

"You're right," Jafar said. "But in this case, no business activity is being conducted in the owner's name either."

"How would you know?" Mona was irritated by Jafar's condescending manner. "He goes to work every day."

"Mona, please understand that whatever I'm telling you is completely true and has been fully verified by our lawyer. I'd never have thought of hurting you by telling you a falsehood."

Mona now noticed Jafar's earnest expression. It made her pause.

"It was all a lie, Mona! All a lie!" Hina said.

Mona turned on her. "So what are you telling me? That Salamat Ali told me a lie about his business? That he—" She stopped. All kinds of scenarios began to occur to her. Was there another woman? A mistress? But what did it have to do with the lawyer?

"Let me finish, Hina," Jafar said, and turned to Mona. "Salamat Ali is bankrupt. He filed for bankruptcy years ago."

"Bankruptcy?" Mona raised her voice. "What bankruptcy?" She could not fully comprehend what Jafar meant.

"You remember," Hina spoke, "what I told you about Salamat Ali's evasive manner when I asked him about his finances? What a fool I was. I should've realized then that there was something fishy."

"Hina, please. Let me tell Mona everything."

"Everything?" Mona laughed nervously. "You haven't told me *everything* yet?"

"I'm coming to it," Jafar said.

"Wait a moment," said Mona. She was now sure that this was not about another woman. "I can save you the rest of it. You're suggesting, with all this proof or whatever it is you have, that Salamat Ali had opportunistic motives in marrying me? And naturally you expect me to believe it. Don't you, Hina? Why did I always sense hostility in you towards Salamat Ali? You were looking to find some blemish in him. That was why you went unannounced to Mrs. Baig's house behind my back to conduct a surprise interview. Don't think I didn't understand your motives—"

"Mona!" Hina protested.

"You're so arrogant in your little conceits that you have no consideration even for my happiness. Remember, we're supposed to be sisters. But no, you had to be proven right in the stupid opinion you've formed of Salamat Ali, no matter what the cost. It had become an ego issue for you. But why? Am I to understand that you're jealous of me? With all your protestations about caring for me, how am I supposed to contend with this notion? Do what you want but don't think even for a moment that I'll sit and hear any more of this. All I can see is that you've found a new pretext to slander him. I want a stop to your meddling in my life." Mona's voice trembled with anger.

"You are wrong," Hina said.

"Mona," Jafar continued, disregarding her outburst, "Salamat Ali had to sell his house to settle with the company that had employed him some years ago. He had, I'm sorry to tell you, embezzled funds kept in trust. He kept protesting his innocence, but the charge was proved in court. Because some of his superiors were sympathetic, he was offered a reprieve if he restored the money. He had to sell his wife's house because by then he had already gambled away all the money he had embezzled. He's a compulsive gambler, Mona. You should know that. There're other details of the case, too, which are equally unpleasant. He was negligent in his first wife's care, too, because of his gambling habit. Most of the time there was no money in the house even for medicines and she did not receive the treatment she should have had. All that information came out when his creditors got wind of the case. His wife's brother had also loaned him money because he was told it was for his sister's treatment. Salamat Ali declared bankruptcy to get rid of his debts but I'm afraid compulsive gamblers are like incurable addicts. The recent pattern of events suggests he has not given up the habit."

Mona listened to Jafar. She was looking at him but at this moment was not conscious of his presence, only of a voice out of a void.

When she finally broke her silence, Mona's tone was defiant.

"I don't believe you, Jafar. I don't believe a word of these lies that you and your wife have cooked up."

Hina could not hold back. "How dare you!"

Jafar gestured to her to remain silent. His voice was calm. "We aren't asking you to believe either of us, Mona. Here's the file with copies of all the relevant documents, including Salamat Ali's own statement, his brother-in-law's witness statement, and the decision written by the judge with the details of the settlement. Please read it."

Jafar got up, leaving the file on the sofa by Mona's side. Hina seemed to want to say something, but Jafar led her away.

Mona stared at the file for a long time.

MONA DID NOT STOP crying for half an hour after reading the file. When she did, she remained in a state of shock. In the beginning, she had tried to convince herself that there had been some mistake, that it was all untrue. She felt as if the news was about someone else, as if it was not herself but a stranger whose life had been torn up by these revelations. She realized that Salamat Ali would be having his breakfast at this moment and waiting for her return for the drive to Hyderabad. She knew just how much more difficult her life was about to become. Sooner or later, everyone would hear the news. She was more worried about the effect it would have on Tanya and Amber than on herself. After inviting the family's censure on the marriage, and making her daughters feel uneasy, how would she bear now the complacent looks of all those who had opposed her? How could she now face Tanya?

Hina came in with a glass of water. She was alone. Mona's eyes filled up with tears again when she saw her sister. "How did you find out?" she asked.

"Umar Shafi first brought it to Jafar's attention."

"Umar Shafi? What did he have to do with it?"

"He had met Salamat Ali before. At Mrs. Baig's house."

"What was he doing there? I don't understand."

"From what I gathered, nobody answered at your house when he had brought that famous cake with the strawberry syrup dedication. Thinking that you might be at Mrs. Baig's, he went there to give it to you. Salamat Ali answered the door and—well, you know how Salamat Ali used to dress. Umar Shafi took him for someone who worked for Mrs. Baig. He left the cake with him with instructions to give it to you when you returned. That was why Umar Shafi was so surprised to see Salamat Ali at our party as the prospective bridegroom. That was also the reason Salamat

Ali picked on him—because he knew Umar Shafi was interested in you." Hina smiled sadly. "And since Umar Shafi had worked in the Accountant General's Office, he found out all he wanted to know about Salamat Ali."

Hina embraced her sister. "Don't cry any more, Mona. Now you know the worst. You'll have to take stock of the situation. For your own sake. You have to be very strong in the days to come."

After a few minutes, Jafar came in with a cup of chamomile tea for Mona and sat down with them. Jafar and Hina watched Mona. Her sister and brother-in-law exchanged glances a few times. Finally, Hina spoke: "We're entirely to blame in this, Mona. Jafar felt terrible when he found out. If only we'd been a little more diligent. When we checked Salamat Ali's personal references, the only people we contacted were those whose names he had given us. Of course, they were in the know and lied to us. We ought to have checked his business history and spoken to other people in his first wife's family—poor woman! How terrible. There's nothing that can be done about it now. But that doesn't mean that you're in any danger or that there's no way out."

Hina paused.

Mona's head was resting on her knees and she did not raise it.

Hina carried on. "Knowing what we know of him, there will be no point at all in asking for a divorce."

Mona looked up. "Divorce? What do you mean?"

"Yes, we're sure that he'll plainly refuse to divorce you," Hina said. "He must be quite hardened by now, after his exposure to the court and the near miss with the jail term. Also, we don't want the stigma of *him* divorcing *you*. The application must be filed by you yourself, terminating the arrangement by giving up your right to the one million rupees he owes you in marriage money. Jafar's lawyer will take care of everything."

"Divorce?" Mona repeated softly to herself. Then she was quiet.

"It'll be a small sacrifice," Hina continued with greater confidence, "compared to how you might end up if this goes on. In all likelihood that money you gave him was also gambled away."

"I want to go home," Mona said abruptly, getting up.

Hina looked at Jafar, who rose quickly.

"Mona," he said, "don't you think it would be better for you to come and spend a few days with us? I'll talk to Salamat Ali. I'm sure I'll be able to make him see reason, and once we're agreed on the terms, he'll be asked to leave the house and you could return to your house."

"For now I just want to go home," Mona repeated.

"That's fine," Hina said, looking at Jafar. "I'll give you a ride. Jafar will call his lawyer again today and ask him to prepare the paperwork. We have a copy of your marriage contract in our safe. All the details that we need are already there. When the matter is taken care of we will bring you here for a few days. Right, Jafar?"

"Yes, that would make more sense," Jafar said. "We don't want to cause any alarm at this stage. Hina will check on you every now and then to make sure that you're okay and safe."

"You're sure you don't want to stay for lunch?" Hina asked.

Mona shook her head and left the room.

Hina conferred with Jafar for a few seconds and then followed her outside.

They did not speak on the ride home.

"It would be better to say nothing to him," Hina said, as Mona was getting out of the car.

Mona closed the door behind her without replying.

Hina waited for a few minutes after Mona had gone inside. Then she drove away.

When Mona walked in, Salamat Ali was in the dining room finishing his breakfast and Habib was brewing another cup of tea.

"Why did you leave suddenly for Hina's house? Don't you want to get ready? Remember we planned to drive to Hyderabad. It'll be late afternoon by the time we get there."

"Salamat!" She looked at him.

"Yes. What is it?"

"Salamat, please promise me you'll never drink again!" Mona's eyes welled up with tears.

"You're still upset with me for that night?" he said with a laugh. "See, I didn't drink as much last night."

"I want you to promise to give it up altogether!" She suddenly caught him in an embrace.

"No violence please," he teased. "Okay, okay, yes, I promise. Now go, get dressed."

"And no more late nights either."

"No more late nights, either."

"I want you to make a solemn promise to me, Salamat, that you'll never drink again or come home late at night," she said, looking into his eyes. "This is not a joke."

"As God is my witness, I promise to Mona that I won't drink ever again and won't come home late as long as I live. Happy now?" he said. "Come, have this tea now. Habib just made it for me. He'll make me another cup while you get dressed. Have you had your breakfast yet? What did Hina want?"

"Nothing. I brought her purse with me by mistake the other night. I went to return it."

"Who dropped you?"

"Jafar got me a taxi. I told them we were leaving for Hyderabad."

"So we are. So we are," he said, drumming on the table.

UNDER ORDINARY CIRCUMSTANCES, Mona would have enjoyed the trip to Hyderabad. She liked the narrow winding alleys of the bazaars, filled with their aromas of food and spices. But she could not get her mind off the disclosure earlier that day. It hit her with greater impact as the hours passed. Throughout the day, Mona unsuccessfully struggled to find some way to convince herself that what she had been told about Salamat Ali did not matter. Salamat Ali remarked on her continued silence a few times, but each time Mona evaded the truth.

They returned late from Hyderabad. Mona felt weak and tired from her inner struggle and the long drive, and went upstairs to lie down. Salamat Ali had eaten too much sweet *rabri* in Hyderabad and felt he couldn't sleep. He paced up and down in the garden. Mona watched his moving shadow, cast on the bedroom curtains by the low garden lights.

She told herself that no marriage was entirely satisfactory. Salamat Ali's first marriage was a mistake, just like her own. It gave no one the right to make terrible accusations about him. Mona found it unthinkable that if she fell sick he might . . . She could not continue the thought.

In all the time of their marriage his interest in her had not subsided. Wasn't it an indication of the strength of their relationship? So he gambled away some money. It was a vice and he must correct it. It was wrong, but hadn't Akbar Ahmad bribed the administrator of the House Building Finance Corporation to expedite his loan application? Didn't Jafar and Hina do the same? Wasn't that a crime as well, in the eyes of both law and religion? Or was it a crime only if one was caught in the act? Akbar Ahmad and Jafar could have been jailed if they had been caught bribing a government official. Hadn't Salamat Ali paid back the money owed to the company by selling the house? In the end, nobody had lost any money.

When Mona heard Salamat Ali come in, she closed her eyes and pretended to be asleep. He undressed and lay down next to her.

Mona thought of Akbar Ahmad. He would like it if she wrecked this new life that had given her happiness and confidence in herself. Not only would he like it, he would be hoping for it. How could he not? She was undoing his life's work. For thirty years, he had done his best to drain all zest for life from her. How could he bear to see that she had rediscovered the meaning of pleasure, that when she laughed now, it was from joy?

Salamat Ali may have taken her money for gambling, Mona thought, but didn't he think of her in everything? She only had to look at an item in a shop and he bought it for her. So what if it was her own money that he spent so liberally on her? The car and the jewellery he had bought for her before she had spent any money on him. If he had wanted to, he could have spent less on her. Didn't she tell him herself that all that money was also equally his? If anybody had truly loved her he could not have done more. He did it all for her because he felt she was the woman of his life, and he had found her. And as for her feelings for him—wasn't he the man she desired? He only had to give up gambling and learn to manage his finances. It was not as if there was another woman.

She turned towards Salamat Ali.

"I thought you were asleep." Salamat Ali chuckled as he drew her close.

X

A REVELATION

Mona planned to go about her life as if nothing had happened. The moment Salamat Ali left, however, Mrs. Baig called her from the garden and the next moment she entered through the kitchen door.

"I heard from Aneesa and Hina, Mona. Now I know the truth. I've come to apologize. By God, I didn't have the slightest idea about Salamat Ali's past or I'd never have become an intermediary. I know you accepted Salamat Ali's proposal because of our friendship alone. You must know that it came as such a shock to me. How sorry I am, you have no idea."

Mona realized that she would need to abandon the dream that she could pretend nothing had happened, just as she had to give up any thoughts of finding perfect happiness with Salamat Ali. She stared at Mrs. Baig without speaking such that her neighbour had difficulty continuing the conversation. When Mrs. Baig became agitated and started chewing the corner of her sari, Mona finally broke her silence.

"How did you hear?"

"Your aunt Aneesa called last night."

"So the whole world knows about it now, I guess," Mona said.

"I didn't mean to intrude," Mrs. Baig said. "But I blame myself."

"Mrs. Baig, please don't say anything more."

"But your whole life is before you. What will you do now?"

"This is not the end of the world, Mrs. Baig. I know I'll have to be strong. There're so many things that need to be taken care of. There are no easy answers."

"But what have you decided?"

"The decision was made when we got married. We will solve all these problems together. Salamat Ali has . . . He's promised not to gamble again."

Mrs. Baig looked blankly at Mona. She left after Mona declined her offer to speak to Salamat Ali.

The enormity of the issue became clearer to Mona after Mrs. Baig left. It was only a matter of time before Tanya and Amber too heard about this. Her heart sank. She had not considered what she would tell them. Not wishing for Habib to see her cry, she sent him home early.

Then the phone rang. It was Jafar, calling to tell Mona that the message had been delivered to Salamat Ali. Jafar explained that he had acted much sooner than planned because the night before, first Tanya and then Amber had arrived at Hina's house after receiving Aunt Aneesa's call, demanding to know what was going on. Mona had not yet returned from Hyderabad, and Hina and Jafar were already contending with a hysterical Mrs. Baig in the drawing room. Despite having given Jafar his promise to keep the news to himself, Umar Shafi had told Aneesa and Sajid Mir everything. Hina and Jafar decided that any further delay in starting the divorce proceedings would be detrimental to Mona and their family's good name.

Thus Jafar sent his lawyer to meet Salamat Ali at his office. At the last minute, the lawyer suggested to Jafar that it would better serve their purposes if he handed photocopies of the evidence directly to Salamat Ali and informed him that the family desired a meeting with him. Salamat Ali would have just enough time to realize that he would not be able to fight the evidence presented against him or to plead his innocence. Then, when given the option to keep the marriage money he owed Mona, he would see it as a good bargain and leave.

SALAMAT ALI CAME HOME an hour later, carrying the lawyer's file. Hearing him enter and climb the stairs, Mona slowly raised her head from the bed where she lay crying.

The moment their eyes met, she rushed at him, flinging herself at him with the rage that had built inside her.

"Why did you do it?" She shook him by his arm. "Tell me! Why?" The consequences of the disclosure, rather than his actions, infuriated her. They were again being publicly humiliated. And this time her family, too, had to bear the brunt.

"What do you mean?" Salamat Ali grabbed her by the shoulders and stared, speaking with a degree of petulance. "Get a hold of yourself! What is the meaning of all this, tell me? I thought we had put it behind us."

Mona stared at him without comprehending.

"Such humiliation," Salamat Ali said, dropping his hands and turning his back to her. "Just when I thought that you had understood and forgiven me, you send me your family lawyer? A lawyer, for God's sake! Didn't you consider how painful it would be for me to have all those terrible memories brought up again?"

"What do you mean I understood and forgave you?" Mona said. She could not believe her ears.

"Did I or did I not make a full confession to you when we were at the beach house?" he asked. "Or are you going to deny everything?"

"What confession?" Mona's palms were perspiring. "What are you talking about?"

"You know very well what confession I am talking about. I opened up my whole life before you. I told you everything. And now I am served this!" He flung the file onto the bed.

"Salamat!" She began sobbing. "Please, tell me what you're saying. You did not tell me anything. I heard nothing from you about any of this."

"Yes, you did. Stop playing these games. You were the last person I had expected to betray me in this manner. Someone with whom I truly felt in—" He collapsed on the bed and began rubbing his temples.

"Salamat!" Mona was now crying bitterly, covering her

face. "I did not know! I did not know, Salamat! You never told me anything. I swear to God, you didn't."

"Ha!" he said. "How could it be, when I told you everything myself?"

Mona silently shook her head.

She felt him watching her. Then he got up and took a few steps towards her.

"Think hard now, Mona. Do you remember my telling you at the beach house about my first wife and the hardships I faced?"

"Yes, I do," she said, looking up and wiping her tears with her hand. "But not about this."

"That's right. But later, I mean, afterwards, I told you everything, about all my problems. At the end you told me yourself that you forgave me. Don't you remember? Think now, Mona!"

"I think . . . I think you said something about—" She struggled simultaneously with her emotions and a forgotten memory.

He came closer. "Yes, tell me what you remember."

Mona recalled that he had said something about forgiveness, but she could not remember the context. She had been drunk, and she had only a vague recollection of the details of that evening.

"I can't remember anything clearly," she said. "I was drunk."

"Wait a minute!" he exclaimed. "Oh my God!" He began walking up and down the room excitedly.

"What is it? What is it, Salamat?" Mona clutched his arm to stop his pacing. She was feeling weak and exhausted.

"Oh, Mona! Something has just occurred to me." Salamat Ali led her by the hand to the bed, where he sat beside her. "Listen, there can be only one explanation: that because you were drunk, you do not recall what I said. I can understand how that could happen. It was the first time you were drinking. It was my mistake—I gave you a little too much, perhaps. Then there's the other possibility: the loud music might have drowned out my words. Can you see how that could happen?"

Mona did not know what to say. Her memory of their conversation at the beach was confused.

Salamat Ali closed his eyes. "I told you, Mona, that I did gamble sometimes. An occasional vice. As far as my business is concerned, yes, I confess, it's not registered. I did it to avoid paying taxes for a few years. You've seen how it is. It's a daily struggle. Money is hard to come by these days and I can't expose my tiny profits to taxes." Salamat Ali opened his eyes and looked at her. "Is it coming to you now?"

Mona did not know what to make of it all. It was true that she had not been in full control of her senses after drinking liquor that night. Was her judgment so impaired that she would not remember such an important conversation? It was the first time she had been drunk.

"I feel so ashamed I suspected you of betraying me, Mona. I am sorry if I seemed upset when I came in. I was sad and angry. I kept asking myself how my Mona could ever do that to me. But now we have an explanation how it all came about. Now I must apologize all over again. I can only hope that just as you forgave me the first time—or as I assumed you did, since you said so at the beach house—you will find it in your heart to forgive me again."

Salamat Ali was gently rubbing her arms.

Mona had never felt so confused.

"What about your wife's illness and her care?" Mona asked after a moment.

"I deny any negligence in my wife's care," he barked. "That's a hundred per cent slander. As soon as I have the resources to hire a lawyer, I'll sue them for maligning my name. I will! I won't let them get away with it. You'll see!"

"But your brother-in-law?" Mona's voice had softened a little. In that one matter, at least, Mona could not bring herself to dispute his account.

"My brother-in-law saw an opportunity. I did take a loan from him once, but it was promptly returned. I only made the mistake of trusting him and not asking him for a receipt when I returned it. Greed makes monsters of people. God help those who fall into their power. They lose the last vestiges of their humanity, these vultures."

The shock, the disbelief and the likelihood that his account was completely true—all this was too much for Mona. She left the room, utterly confused and doubting her own senses and judgment.

That evening while Mona was sitting in the living room pretending to read a magazine, she could hear Salamat Ali pacing in the corridor. Suddenly she heard him curse Umar Shafi, and the next moment he barged into the room. "Umar Shafi is a lowlife and a trouble-maker," Salamat Ali shouted. "He will hear from me, rest assured!"

He stood staring at Mona for a few moments, and when she did not answer, he left the room.

Minutes later, she heard him leave the house.

Mona's first thought was that Salamat Ali might confront Umar Shafi and do something rash. She wondered how Salamat Ali had recognized Umar Shafi's hand in the matter. She had not told him the name of the source.

But that was followed by a feeling of relief that she had been left alone.

SALAMAT ALI RETURNED a few hours later. He looked calm. Mona did not hear him mention Umar Shafi again that day or in the days that followed. But despite the explanations offered by Salamat Ali about the beach incident, Mona remained uneasy. For his part, Salamat Ali acted as if they had already reached a rapprochement. He did not discuss the matter again with her. Instead, he took her out to dinner three days in a row and tried to persuade her to go on a vacation with him. While the issue was far from being over for Mona, she realized that if she announced her acceptance of Salamat Ali's version of the events for now, it could very well provide her with a way out of her dilemma on her own terms. Everything had happened too fast: the disclosure by Hina and Jafar, Salamat Ali's revelation to her, and the legal action carried out by Hina and Jafar—which she felt was as much aimed at rescuing her as it was intended to substantiate their opinion of Salamat Ali.

Just as she had finally begun to gain some control over her life, it was coming apart. She needed time to think everything through. After all that had transpired, she told

herself, there was nothing she could lose by giving herself
some time to obtain a clear view of her situation. She felt so
irate at everyone around her that she did not even care
about the immediate consequences of her actions for herself, let alone how others might interpret them.

The next time Salamat Ali asked her to come out for
dinner with him, Mona suddenly said, "I don't want you to
be present at the meeting with the lawyer. The fault is
mine. I am unable to recall those moments when you told
me all you say you did."

Salamat Ali looked strangely at her but said nothing.
There was something in Mona's manner that belied this
seemingly calm acceptance of Salamat Ali's version of
events. It was not lost on him. He looked confused and
unsure. He tried to pull her towards him to embrace her,
but Mona stood stiffly with her arms by her sides.

THEY WERE GATHERED around the table in Mona's dining
room. Jafar's lawyer, Barrister Huda, also practised family
law. He sat quietly for some time, hands interlocked on
the table, then shifted in his chair and glanced around the
table at Mona, Jafar and Hina.

Hina asked Mona, "Where is Salamat Ali?"

"He will not be coming," Mona said.

"Will not be coming?" Huda repeated in a heavy, pon-
derous voice.

"What do you mean he will not be coming?" Hina asked.
"Didn't you tell him that we would be meeting today?"

Mona did not reply.

"Well, if he wants to stay out of it, that's his choice," Jafar said. "His presence is not really needed here. Mona can tell him about our discussions later."

At a nod from Jafar, Barrister Huda removed a file from his briefcase.

"If you have any questions, I'll do my best to answer them," he said, handing Mona a copy.

Mona glanced over the paper. "All the information seems to be here. All entered correctly, too," she murmured. Her fingers moved nervously along the edges of the printed sheets.

Hina regarded her silently.

"If you have any questions—" Huda reminded her.

"There are no questions," Mona said. "There are none. There's been a complete misunderstanding."

Hina and Jafar looked at her. Barrister Huda only raised an eyebrow.

"Misunderstanding about what?" he asked.

"About this whole thing. I had forgotten. I had forgotten that Salamat Ali had already told me everything about his past."

Hina looked incredulously at Jafar and then turned towards Mona, who now looked defiantly back at her. Barrister Huda looked at Jafar, who turned towards Hina.

Leaning forward on the table Huda asked Mona, "Are you saying that you have changed your mind about initiating these proceedings?"

Mona nodded without looking at him.

"But this is preposterous!" Hina burst out. "Mona, what is this man doing to you?"

"What is all this, Mona?" Jafar asked sternly.

Mona smiled faintly to herself.

"Just hold it one moment," said Huda. "Mrs. Mona Salamat Ali, have you fully considered the consequences of your statement? Because if what you just said now is true, there's no purpose in my presence here. There is no cause."

"There is no cause, indeed," Mona said.

"Mona!" Hina said with a sense of urgency. "Tell him! Tell him that you want the divorce. Tell him your decision."

"I just did." Mona pushed away the paper. "Stop telling me what to do with my life."

THE LAWYER LEFT after a brief, private conversation with Jafar. After listening to Mona's account, Hina and Jafar sat silent for a moment.

"What a crafty—" Jafar did not finish. He clenched his fists.

"Now I'm really afraid about your safety, Mona," Hina said. "How could you fall for something like that? It was all premeditated. Clearly he set it up so that he could fool you."

"He cares for me. That's all I know."

"He does not!" Hina laughed derisively.

"How can you say that?" Mona said in a flat tone.

"How can you even think he loves you and cares for you?" Hina said. "With all this evidence, too."

Mona fell silent again. Her obstinate look had returned.

"I'll be at home, Hina," Jafar said, getting up. "When you're ready you can call me and I'll come and pick you up."

Mona turned her face away to avoid looking at him.

"There's no hurry to sign these papers, Mona, if you want more time to consider," Jafar said. "I brought Barrister Huda today only because I thought we had already agreed on the course of action. Naturally, it cannot be an easy decision when one has been wronged so gravely, but it'll be easier to live with, I'm sure, than the prospect of continuing with this arrangement. Particularly now, after everyone in the family has learned the truth about Salamat Ali. They'll ask why Mona wishes to remain in such a relationship. There can be no reasonable answer to that."

"Who is the family to decide what I must or mustn't do?" Mona demanded, looking at Hina.

"No one is forcing you," Hina said. "You alone will have to make the decision."

"Too many people have tried to run my life with their expectations," Mona said. "You asked me to get rid of Akbar Ahmad, too, in the same manner. Maybe I should have done it, but I didn't. And when you saw that I was happy to carry on, you accepted my decision. He was always treated with respect in your house. When I tell you now that I don't wish to proceed with this divorce, why can't you accept that? Or is it again the same problem which you seem to have with Salamat Ali? Good only for running errands but not good enough to be shown respect as a family member?"

Hina exchanged looks with Jafar. "I think I will take a short walk," he said, and left the room.

"How do you feel about that now?" Hina said.

"Feel about what?"

"About Akbar Ahmad and the mistake you made in his case."

"I feel I was cheated out of my life. I'm not ashamed to admit it. But how bad is Salamat Ali's crime? Is it any worse than the thousand little hypocrisies we live with in our daily lives? Even if one assumes that his account of events is untrue—which we cannot be sure about—all that Salamat Ali is guilty of is hiding his past as far as it concerns our relationship. He hasn't wronged me in any other way. Even if everything they say about this case is true, I shall not consider divorce yet. And that case against him. All I'll ever say is that the manner in which Akbar Ahmad amassed his savings at my expense was a far worse crime than any embezzling anyone could ever do. You fought with him too, I agree, but you never persecuted him with the single-mindedness you have shown in Salamat Ali's case. If you care so much about my suffering that you can disregard my own choices for my life, why didn't you and Jafar descend on Akbar Ahmad with Barrister Huda and divorce papers? What has changed? I had said no then and I am saying no now. Even if there was some financial wrongdoing as has been alleged in this case, it was corrected and is now a thing of the past. Why are *you* bothered when *I* am willing to live with it? What is in it for you? Or does it all boil down to the same old issues you have had with Salamat Ali from the beginning, and the chance you see now for a vendetta in the guise of forcing a divorce?"

Hina was startled by Mona's sudden outburst. Jafar quietly entered the room. Mona realized he had been listening in the corridor.

"But how can you be happy with him after you know all these horrible details?" he said. "How can you trust a man who has a history like that? You won't always feel so young. Do you want to live with someone against whom you have to be constantly on your guard?"

"I'm the one who is taking the risk!"

"But your daughters—" Jafar said.

"I've already given them their share of the inheritance. They have nothing to lose."

"I didn't mean that, Mona!" Jafar said. "What I meant was that they have their in-laws to deal with. Please think about the awkward situation they already find themselves in. It'll only worsen if you don't get rid of Salamat Ali."

"How excellent, Jafar. Now you're sounding just like Uncle Sajid Mir. He threatened me under this roof that he would have Salamat Ali arrested. Why do all of you think you can treat me and my husband in such an offhand manner? It's his house, too. Please don't forget that."

Jafar's face turned red. "I never—"

"I do have a right as your sister to see that you don't suffer a worse fate than you did the first time," Hina said sternly. "If you want to make a fool of yourself, at least don't try to malign our intentions. Just remember that both Jafar and I supported you in your decision to marry this man."

"Even though we didn't think it was a wise choice," Jafar interjected.

Hina cast a disapproving glance at Jafar for the interruption and continued, "We are using the same right that we used earlier to defend your actions before the rest of the family. Only this time, it's to dissuade you from folly which would be obvious if you only opened your eyes. If you don't want to divorce him, fine! But remember you'll have only yourself to blame if anything goes wrong."

"And from what we have already learned of him," Jafar put in, "don't count on it that it won't. As far as I know he has never uttered a word of apology or regret."

"He made an apology to me." Mona said. "That's enough. He does not have to make a single apology to anybody else in the whole world."

Even as she said these words Mona wondered if what Salamat Ali had said to her constituted an apology. Was he remorseful? Was it really an apology, or only a pretext so that Mona would not be upset with him?

Jafar spoke after what seemed a long silence. "You don't need us to tell you that we have your best interests at heart. You aren't some adolescent who cannot be reasoned with, Mona. See the facts for yourself: here is someone who misled us about his character and married you under what anyone would regard as false pretenses. Then there's all the money he's been borrowing from you in the name of his business without you keeping any account of it."

"Forget about the money you already spent," Hina said. "We know he's a compulsive gambler. If you think you're helping him, you are mistaken."

"You should get some rest now, Mona," Jafar said. "And think everything over carefully. Keep this paper with you and give us a call if you want to see us at any time about this matter. Barrister Huda's number is on the letterhead. You can talk to him about any detail of the matter in complete confidence—even about issues which you might not feel comfortable discussing with us." As he left, Jafar put the papers near Mona who sat without answering and stared at the documents in front of her. She did not say anything or move. Jafar made a gesture to Hina to get up. Hina's hands rested for a moment on Mona's shoulders before she left.

As she heard the gate close and the car drive away, Mona broke into sobs. She was overwhelmed by the feeling that in her effort to thwart Hina and Jafar's machinations, she may have foreclosed her options by taking too rigid a stance, especially since she was still unsure of her own future course of action. She blamed Hina for forcing her into a situation where she had compromised her own interests.

SALAMAT ALI RETURNED after Hina and Jafar left. When Mona heard him enter the house she quickly dried her eyes. Salamat Ali picked up the paper from the table and came towards her.

He tried to kiss her, but she turned her face away.

"Are you still angry with me?" he asked.

Mona did not answer.

He appeared thoughtful for a second.

"You're right," he said. "We need some time to forget about this whole unpleasant business. And we will. I know what we'll do. We'll go to a nice restaurant this evening and bury all these bad memories. I'll do any penance you suggest. I owe it to you, yes, I do."

"I don't feel like going to a restaurant today," Mona said without looking at him.

"Then we can have some food delivered from a restaurant. What do you like, chicken roast, shish kebabs? I know—you've never told me but I know you really like bihari kebabs. Isn't that true?" He held her chin and tried to turn her face towards him. "Tell me."

"I'll be spending the night at Amber's house." Mona took a step away from him. "I told her I'll come over tonight. Kamal is coming to pick me up."

"Oh, no, Mona! No! Tell them you've changed your mind." Salamat Ali tried to take her into his arms. "Really, I wanted so much to spend this evening with you. Just you and me. We have gone through some very difficult moments together recently. I wanted to—"

"Salamat, please don't!" She turned towards him.

He released her immediately.

"As you wish, Mona. As you wish. I was just saying . . . I'll be happy with whatever makes you happy."

Salamat Ali studied Mona's face for some time and then quietly withdrew.

WHEN KAMAL CAME to pick up Mona, Salamat Ali was upstairs in the bedroom and did not come down to see her off.

Observing Mona's quiet expression, Kamal did not initiate any conversation or exchange more than a few words with her on the way to his and Amber's house.

Mona tried to reason with herself. Even if Hina and Jafar were right, and Salamat Ali had some interest in her money, what difference did it make? Did she care? Didn't women often marry financially secure men? Then again, someone who had wished only to deceive her with false expressions of love to obtain her money would not have gone to the lengths Salamat Ali had to surprise her with the jewellery and saris, would he? If Salamat Ali was so calculating, he would have seen that she was vulnerable. He could have convinced her of his devotion without much effort. How could Hina and Jafar be right?

As the houses and shops paraded past the car window, Mona told herself that even if her recent feelings were a delusion, they were by far preferable to the thirty years of immaculate deception she had suffered in her first marriage. Yet she had to forgive Akbar Ahmad—perhaps because he was already dead. It should not be too hard for her to forget the petty misdemeanours of someone who had not emotionally wounded her, but who nevertheless seemed to care for her. Wouldn't forgiving Salamat Ali be easier because he was, until recently, the source of a happiness she had thought was not meant for her? That sense, even if it became a memory now, would remain the most precious part of her life. Mona had asked herself before, too, if it was possible that more than fearing the loss of Salamat Ali, she was frightened to lose the feelings she had discovered through his presence in her life. She had not been able to answer the question until now. She had been unable to separate the two in her mind.

By the time Mona arrived at Amber's house, she felt a clear sense of something having changed irreparably in her relationship with Salamat Ali. She could not fully discern it. She was only aware that she felt pity for Salamat Ali, and that in a strange sort of way, this made him unattractive to her.

XI

THE AfTERMATH

After returning from Amber's house and over the next few days, Mona felt abandoned. Tanya suddenly seemed very busy at work, and Hina had not visited her since their last argument over the phone. Salamat Ali never missed an opportunity to remind her how unjustly she was being treated by her family just because she loved him. It grieved Mona that she had no opportunity to contradict him. Sometimes, the manner in which he criticized her family also repelled her. It only made her feel more keenly her family's rejection and her isolation.

Mona told Mrs. Baig that she wished her family were more accommodating of Salamat Ali. Now that she had accepted his apology and explanations, they had no reason to hold any grudges against him.

Mona missed Hina.

"I won't call her," she told herself. "Let her call me first."

When Mrs. Baig invited Mona, Salamat Ali and other family members to her house for lunch on the weekend, Hina did not come. Faraz and Kamal also excused themselves.

"Why didn't Faraz come?" Mrs. Baig asked Tanya when the rest had arrived.

"He had to take his mother for a dental appointment," she answered.

Salamat Ali sniggered. Tanya turned to look at him.

"I thought Mrs. Kazi had very strong teeth," Salamat Ali commented. "Whatever happened to them?"

Tanya gave him a dark look.

Only Amber smiled. Mrs. Baig shook her head.

Mona's face did not show any reaction. Later, when Salamat Ali took her son, Zain, to the veranda to show him the budgerigars, Tanya led him away, telling Mona she was taking the child to her house for a nap.

To divert attention from the snub, Salamat Ali went outside for a smoke.

Amber gave Mona a report on Umar Shafi and Rubab's wedding, which had been celebrated recently. Neither Mona nor anyone from her immediate family had attended. According to the reports that had reached her, the wedding sermon was delayed for almost an hour after Uncle Sajid Mir reneged on his promise to give his house in the dowry. Umar Shafi threatened to call off the wedding. Rubab broke down in hysterics. Aunt Aneesa fainted. Finally a compromise agreement was reached: Umar Shafi and Rubab were to have the upper storey of the house while Sajid Mir and Aneesa would continue living downstairs.

Mona could not help smiling.

~~~

ON TANYA'S FIFTH WEDDING ANNIVERSARY, the newlywed
couple, Rubab and Umar Shafi, had been invited, as Hina
had advised Tanya to extend the invitation to avoid further
tensions and rifts in the family. Mona first thought that
perhaps Hina wanted to make a statement of some sort by
advising Tanya to invite Umar Shafi. Then she remembered that Hina had not attended Umar Shafi's wedding
herself. Mona sensed that Hina really wanted to facilitate
a family reconciliation. If that was indeed the case, Mona
told herself, it would be important for Salamat Ali to
attend the gathering. Still, she thought it best to see what
he himself had to say.

"It's not as if we have done anything wrong that we
should hide from people," Salamat Ali told her. "Of course,
we'll go."

At the gathering, Mona saw Hina but did not speak to her,
although she noticed that Hina smiled at her a few times
when their eyes met. Salamat Ali did not leave Mona's side.

Jafar briefly greeted Mona in passing. She later regretted answering him because he did not greet Salamat Ali.
Mona finally realized that she was mistaken to think that
Hina and Jafar meant to effect a reconciliation with
Salamat Ali. She was mad at Hina but she also felt annoyed
with Salamat Ali, whose presence was distancing her from
her family.

Salamat Ali kept mostly to himself. Everyone noticed
that his usual verve was missing and that he made no jokes
with Faraz or Kamal.

Mona was surprised when Aunt Aneesa greeted her seemingly without any hostile feelings. She was sitting next to her daughter in a corner of the room, where Umar Shafi had just brought Rubab a bowl of chickpea salad.

"There are no potatoes in it!" Rubab said to her mother in alarm, after prodding the contents of the bowl with her spoon. "Why didn't he get me any potatoes?"

"Let me see," Aunt Aneesa said, poking her finger in the bowl. When she had verified that there were indeed no potatoes, she gave Umar Shafi a foul look. Rubab was fast becoming inconsolable. Before the situation could deteriorate, Umar Shafi got up, took the bowl from Rubab's hands and made his way through the guests back to the dining table at the other end of the room.

"Don't forget the sweet sauce!" someone cried out in a shrill voice, just as he had reached the table.

Mona started. She had never heard Rubab raise her voice. Aware of the stares directed her way, Rubab tittered nervously. When she saw Mona smiling, she stopped, and a flash of jealous suspicion lit her face.

Mona suddenly realized that Aunt Aneesa was being kind to her only because she no longer had any reason to resent her existence.

Showing signs of animation for the first time, Salamat Ali made a point of sniggering as Umar Shafi passed by carrying the bowl of chickpeas. Imad arrived late, and Mona noticed that he avoided her. He acknowledged her only with a silent nod. She was hurt; the thought did not comfort her that he was probably keeping away so as not to get into another scene with Salamat Ali. She wished that Imad would come and talk to her, if only for a moment. She did not care what Salamat Ali might say.

LATER IN THE EVENING, Faraz opened the small cabinet where he kept his bar, and the men gravitated to the dining room. Salamat Ali did not move. Mona saw Jafar whisper to Faraz, who went to the dining room and poured a glass of scotch that he took to Jafar.

"Faraz," Mona said in a loud, clear voice, as he passed by on his way to the dining room, "please bring Salamat a drink."

Mrs. Kazi, sitting opposite, looked at Mona in disbelief. Hina stopped in the middle of her conversation with Amber.

Faraz looked first at Salamat Ali, then Mona.

Salamat Ali, too, looked confused. "I . . . I'll go and get it myself."

He made as if to rise, but Mona pressed his arm down.

"No," she said in a calm voice. "Faraz is going to the dining room. He'll get you one."

"Yes, sure! Sure! I'll get it for you." Faraz quickly walked away.

When Faraz brought Salamat Ali his glass of scotch, Mrs. Kazi averted her gaze. He held the drink as Mona continued talking to Salamat Ali.

"Thank you, Faraz." Salamat Ali finally said, taking the glass from his hands.

Mona looked away to suppress a smile.

Salamat Ali was surprised when, after he had taken a sip, Mona quietly asked him to put away the drink.

"But why?" he asked. "Didn't you just ask—?"

"Just put it away!" Mona's tone was resolute.

Salamat Ali did not need to be told again.

ON THE DRIVE HOME, a speeding minibus without headlights forced Salamat Ali to swerve behind a truck. It was the second time Salamat Ali had tried unsuccessfully to overtake the slow-moving truck. The jolt threw Mona to one side and she hit the door.

"Salamat, please, drive carefully! Slow down a bit!" she said as she grasped the overhead handle.

"I know people like them!" he said, without slowing down. "They think they're somebody. They like to think of themselves as sophisticated. What do they know about life? Just because they have a house in Clifton do they think that they're cultured? Nine out of ten houses in Clifton are made from black money. Everyone knows that. Faraz's father was a government supplier. Everyone knows how money is made in that business. And Jafar! He was in federal government. And we all know how clean and uncorrupted *they* are! How did he get all the money on a government servant's salary to make a big house like that? If I wanted, I could also talk. I just keep quiet because I don't want to give them a chance to say anything about you."

Mona felt irritated by Salamat Ali's droning on about her family. She did not even try to defend Jafar, who had inherited his family house.

"I am telling you, Mona."

"Just forget about it," she said, lightly rubbing his shoulder as if he were a child, and realized that her feelings towards him now were almost maternal. "We had a good time, didn't we?"

"That we did." Salamat Ali chuckled. "I was so happy to see Umar Shafi and his loving bride. I was. And I loved the way you got that Faraz to get me a drink in front of his mother. It'll teach them both a nice lesson. But why didn't you let me finish my drink?"

Mona did not reply.

Salamat Ali had finally slowed down.

SALAMAT ALI CAUGHT MONA'S ARM as she switched on the bedroom light and tried to pull her towards him. She turned and faced him.

He must have noticed the expression on her face.

"What?" Salamat Ali said, looking confused and a little nettled. He dropped her arm.

"Nothing," Mona said, looking at him a little coldly. "I'm feeling too tired tonight."

"It's okay," Salamat Ali said sulkily. "If you're tired, you're tired. There's nothing to be done about it."

XII

THE BREACH

Tanya told Mona that she would come over that afternoon. Mona was pensive after receiving her call. What did Tanya wish to see her about? she wondered. Perhaps her daughter had finally realized the grief that her words had caused and wanted to apologize. But no, Mona knew that Tanya never apologized for anything. She only pretended the incident had never happened. Mona had learned to live with her daughter's attitude, though she found it infuriating.

Salamat Ali came home for lunch and overheard Mona talking on the phone to Tanya and planning a visit for the late afternoon. He always went back to work around that time. Today he stayed home.

Mona felt uneasy about his being there. She knew that he was aware of the cooling relationship between mother and daughter. She was relieved, however, that he had no knowledge of their last conflict. Mona could not ask Salamat

Ali to leave the room, and in his presence Tanya would not be able to broach the subject. Mona was grateful to Salamat Ali for his tolerance of Tanya's behaviour, but she was aware that Salamat Ali had tried to annoy her daughter, and Mona particularly wished to avoid any exchange of hostilities between them.

Salamat Ali stayed in the living room watching the cricket match on television, but by the time Tanya arrived, he was bored. He turned the TV off in the middle of the game, to the vexation of Habib, who had been craning his neck every few minutes from the kitchen door to check the action replays. Seeing him leave the room, Mona sat down there with Tanya. However, her relief at Salamat Ali's going away was short-lived. He returned almost immediately, carrying the fruit basket from the kitchen, and sat down at the nearby dining table. Mona felt it was too late for her to take Tanya to another room.

Tanya darted an irritated glance in Salamat Ali's direction. He was peeling an apple with great concentration. Mona waited for Tanya to speak.

Finally Tanya said in an undertone, "I'd like you to come with me tomorrow to see someone."

"Where? Whom?" Mona asked. "What about?" Then she sat up. It suddenly occurred to her that Tanya might be pregnant again.

"A lady lawyer." Tanya had lowered her voice further.

"A lady what?" It took a few moments before she understood what Tanya meant.

"Don't shout now, it's for you. And you know why," Tanya said.

Mona felt enraged. "See a lawyer? Who are you to tell me what to do? Didn't Hina tell you that I don't wish to hear about it?" Mona's voice rose in anger. She momentarily forgot Salamat Ali's presence. "You aren't my mother, I'm yours! How dare you even speak to me without first apologizing!"

"Apologize for what?" Tanya asked.

Salamat Ali brought the plate and placed it on the coffee table. He had peeled, cored and quartered two apples. The pieces were neatly arranged in a circle. He sat down beside Mona.

"Have some apple, Tanya," he said. "You should also have some, Mona."

"No, thank you," Tanya said curtly.

"No need to be like that, Tanya. Apples are good for the brain. It'll help you understand the situation a little better."

"I'm not talking to you!" Tanya snapped.

"Yes, Tanya. I understand that. You aren't talking to me. You are talking to your mother, who happens to be my wife, about something which concerns me. I'm also aware that I hold the relationship of a father to you, whether or not you care to acknowledge it."

Tanya raised her hand indignantly. "Please spare me this melodrama! My father is dead and you of all people will never take his place."

"As you wish," Salamat Ali said, picking up an apple slice and nibbling on it, while looking at Mona out of the corner of his eye. "I've no desire to force myself on you as a father, but one thing you *must* understand, Tanya . . ." His tone changed.

Something in it made Tanya sit up straighter.

"Your mother and I made a decision to get married, and we did. We didn't intrude upon anyone else's life, and we didn't create any problems for anyone. People have their problems, I understand that. Sometimes these problems are work-related as it is in my case, and sometimes these problems are related to one's spouse and in-laws. There're as many problems as there're people. I don't wish to get into details about your life. All I'm saying is that, just as Mona and I are trying to solve our problems between ourselves and endeavouring to build a life together, maybe you should also do the same."

"I don't want to hear you commenting about my life and family," Tanya hissed.

"No? Really? Then how can I allow you to comment on *my* life and family?"

"I was discussing an important issue with my mother."

"Your mother is my wife and the *issue* you were discussing is directly related to me. Or are you going to lie to your own mother's face, Tanya, and tell me that you didn't just ask her to consult a divorce lawyer? If that doesn't concern me, I don't know what does! Yes, there were some unfortunate things that happened in the past. Mona was unhappy about them. *I* was unhappy about them. Hina and Jafar felt some concern and suggested a recourse. We explained our position to them and they understood. Mrs. Baig understood. Everyone understood—including your sister, Amber. Only you didn't understand, Tanya. I had to ask myself why it was that, despite my best efforts, you always maintained the same offensive attitude towards me.

I have come to the conclusion that perhaps it's because of some deep-seated unhappiness you feel about your own marital relationship, Tanya."

Tanya cast a wounded look at Mona, as if she felt betrayed by her mother's continued silence. Though Mona did not agree with what Salamat Ali said, she did not intervene. The frustration of her own bitter dealings with Tanya made her feel that her daughter almost deserved to hear those harsh words. As a mother, Mona could not speak every thought that crossed her mind, but she reasoned to herself that others would not put up with Tanya's nonsense as she had.

Salamat Ali smiled at Tanya and continued, "Though I don't know what it could be. Faraz looks healthy enough to me."

"Shut your filthy mouth!" Tanya screamed.

"Salamat, no!" Mona cried.

"I rest my case," Salamat Ali said, unaffectedly.

"Stop it both of you!" Mona was shocked and horrified. She now wished she had intervened sooner, before the argument took this undignified turn.

"I also happen to know a thing or two about life, Mona!" Salamat Ali continued. "A daughter unhappy with her married life could resent her own mother's happiness. I'm saying this because Tanya is not a child. She finds herself qualified enough to prescribe divorce for you, her own mother, against your wishes. I'll no longer sit here and listen to her make these shameless suggestions to you. I'll take steps, rest assured!"

"And what might those be?" Tanya asked mockingly. There was a menacing look on her face.

"Salamat, that's enough. I don't wish this to continue!" Mona said. She had no desire to let Salamat Ali get embroiled in her already complicated and delicate relationship with her daughter. Mona could see Tanya getting ready to retaliate, her expression hardening. Mona wished to put an end to the confrontation before either of them went any further.

Salamat Ali was charged up. "No, Mona, let me speak!" he said. "I feel I've a right to defend my name and honour against vile persecution. I don't care for an apology from you for myself, Tanya, but I can say with confidence that your mother will no longer welcome you here, until you apologize to her for making these suggestions."

"Stop this, Salamat!" Mona finally screamed. "Stop it! I told you that was enough!"

Salamat Ali looked shocked at Mona's reaction. Something did not seem to make sense to him.

Tanya laughed derisively. Her face was distorted with hatred, which she directed as much at her mother as at Salamat Ali.

"You can't make me apologize for anything, let me tell you that, Mr. Salamat Ali," Tanya said. "And this, in case you don't realize, is *my* home! The person who can forbid me from visiting here is not born yet. Just remember that." She walked up to the dining table, pulled out a chair and sat down at the head of the table, glaring defiantly at Salamat Ali.

"Mona!" Salamat Ali turned towards her.

"Yes, ask her if she can stop me from coming here!" Tanya said.

"Leave me alone, all of you! I won't let any of you manipulate me," Mona shouted and stomped out of the room.

Pretending to follow Mona, Salamat Ali also left.

Tanya's eyes welled up with tears. She absent-mindedly picked up one of the apples from the fruit basket and sank her teeth into it.

DESPITE ALL THE ANGER and consternation Mona had felt at Tanya's attitude in the past, once again she felt plagued by guilt for remarrying. She felt that she had done an injustice to her daughters by so doing. Her unravelling relationship with Salamat Ali kept reinforcing that guilt. The more furiously Tanya retaliated against any imagined wrong now, the more remorseful Mona felt. She also noticed a pronounced sneer on Akbar Ahmad's face every time she passed by the portrait. She found it inescapable.

The encounter between Tanya and Salamat Ali had made Mona apprehensive. She knew that if there were to be other such scenes in the future involving her, she could not avoid taking sides. Regardless of her unsatisfactory relationship with Tanya, she could not imagine compromising it for Salamat Ali's sake. But she also didn't want Tanya to feel she could take advantage of her feelings or exploit them in any conflict with Salamat Ali.

MONA NOTICED SALAMAT ALI becoming more cantankerous by the day in his dealings with the servants. The new maidservant had already left the job after he had shouted at her.

Two days later, Salamat Ali abused Habib in Mona's presence for putting too much salt in the curry. The servants had never been ill-treated in her family. She did not say anything to him in front of Habib, but as Salamat Ali was getting ready to go out for the evening, she brought up the subject.

He listened for a moment, then projected a shower of expletives. "So he complained to you, did he?"

Mona also raised her voice. "Please don't use such language, Salamat! You are speaking to me, just remember that. He didn't complain. You said those things to him in my presence. I'm telling you now because I didn't wish to bring up this matter in front of him."

"The other day I caught him watching TV in the living room. What was he doing there?"

"He was watching TV after finishing his work. If you have an objection to his sitting in the living room, I'll talk to him. But I don't like your hostile behaviour towards the servants in this house. They aren't used to this kind of treatment."

"They're all bastards and like to shirk their duties! The only language they understand is slaps and kicks! I know them very well. I don't want them to think that they can do as they please in this house. I'll keep a strict watch on them."

Salamat Ali spun around and left the room.

Mona was disgusted by his behaviour. She had accepted his unpolished manners, but the sudden and vulgar display of his small-mindedness completely shocked her.

In the beginning, she had tolerated his ill temper because she thought that the anxiety and humiliation from the disclosure of Salamat Ali's past and his continued business worries was its cause. She now found his temper inexcusable. She feared that if he went any further, Salamat Ali would lose all remaining respect from the servants as well.

SALAMAT ALI HAD NOT DISCUSSED his business recently with Mona, but when he was unusually quiet over meals for a couple of days, Mona asked him if something bothered him. He shook the newspaper to remove a crease and turned away.

"It's just that all the talking and investigations have had a bad influence on my reputation in the bank where I have my account," he said. "They're refusing to issue me a letter of credit for a consignment I have to order."

"How did the bank find out?" Mona said.

"How do you think? Jafar's lawyer had gone there to make inquiries about me. These things don't remain hidden. Rather than going behind my back in this manner, if they had directly asked me to show them my accounts, I wouldn't be in this mess now."

Mona realized that this might well be true. Even a hint of trouble could adversely prejudice business relationships with the banks. If Jafar's lawyer had asked questions about Salamat Ali, the bank could easily have become suspicious and denied him credit. Knowing this made her feel the guilt of the wrong done to Salamat Ali.

"I'm sorry about it," Mona said. "How much is it that you need?"

"I'm not sure," he said.

Their eyes met. She knew he was lying and she hoped that he would stop and not say another word. She desperately hoped for a sign that he wanted to redeem himself.

"I don't need the money all at once," Salamat Ali said. "For the first month, just fifty thousand rupees will be enough."

"What consignment is it?" Mona asked unhappily.

"A new variety of paper I wanted to import. Very high profit margins. Very high."

She gave him the money.

Mona told herself she could not have refused, but she disliked her own weakness in the face of his exploitation, and in making excuses for it to herself. She wondered how this would end. How long would it take him to gamble away the funds? She tried to tell herself that this time he really needed the money, but she was not convinced. The look in his eye had told her all she needed to know.

"Thank you, Mona," Salamat Ali said, putting the cheque she had written in his briefcase. "You've been my only support in this turbulent period. You have shown me the trust that only true love inspires. Without you I wouldn't have survived. This time for sure I'll return this loan within a few months. There'll be a good profit, too."

She winced and wished he had not spoken those words, which degraded him further in her eyes.

Salamat Ali left the room to make a phone call.

Mona felt resentment at Salamat Ali's abusing the feelings she had had for him. There was a time when she felt that he cared for her. But if he had really cared about her feelings, wouldn't he have given up gambling for her sake? Mona considered the change she had undergone herself when she felt she was the centre of his attention. She had hoped to be the centre of his emotions, too, but that had not proved to be the case.

Mona also asked herself why she had no influence on Salamat Ali's life in a like manner. Why wasn't her presence worth anything to him? It was possible that gambling was his refuge from the problems of his first marriage, but why did he continue when he was with her? If he did not fully understand the difficulties she had overcome to be with him, was he also blind to the fact that after the scandal broke, she had stood by him and taken everyone's rebukes for his sake? Yet, he had not changed. He had not even tried. Did he love her? Did he even care about her?

She wondered if it were an illusion, too, that Salamat Ali's presence in her life had brought her happiness. What if inside she had always been the person she was now, and had recovered her lost self when Akbar Ahmad's shadow was lifted from her? Hina had said as much when Jafar teased her about her new, younger look. There was a pall that had hung over her existence for a long time after Akbar Ahmad's death. What was it? The sense that her life had been wasted, or that she would not struggle to find happiness for herself as readily as she was willing to sacrifice herself for others? In the end, Mona could not deny that whatever its nature, the pall was cast away only when her relationship with Salamat Ali reintroduced her to the joy of being alive.

When Salamat Ali returned, he was dressed to go out. "I'll take you shopping for clothes this afternoon. Then we'll have lunch out."

"I have enough clothes for now, Salamat," Mona said.

"Not this month."

"Let's have lunch outside, then," he said. "My treat."

"Amber is coming today," Mona said. "I promised to make kofta curry for her. She'd been asking me for it for a long time."

"What's wrong with you? Before you didn't make all these excuses when I asked you to come out with me," he said.

"Salamat, there's no reason to be upset." Mona remained calm. "We can go for lunch tomorrow. I won't make any other plans."

"As you wish," he said testily, and walked away.

She was relieved to see him go.

THE COOK WAS WORKING NOISILY in the kitchen when Mona came down for breakfast. Mona soon understood the reason for his enthusiasm when Mrs. Baig telephoned to say that her old maidservant Noori had been sitting out-side her gate for half an hour, Mona went outside.

"Why didn't you knock?" Mona said.

"I didn't have the courage, Mona bibi!" Noori said.

"Come inside. You should have knocked. I was wonder-ing if you'd come."

"How could I not come, Mona bibi, when you called me?"

"Habib told me that you aren't working anywhere. Is that true?'

"My youngest son was not well. I took him to work but they sent me away and said I should leave him at home. I couldn't do that. When he got well and I went back, they told me they'd hired somebody else."

"When can you start?" Mona asked.

"I came ready to work today, Mona bibi," she said, lowering her eyes.

"You remember where all the cleaning things are kept?"

"Yes, Mona bibi!"

"The rooms haven't been cleaned for a week now. Sweep and mop them first before doing any other work."

"The bedroom, too, Mona bibi?" She looked concerned.

"Yes, the bedroom too," Mona said, looking away. "You can start now!"

Mona turned to go away.

"Mona bibi!"

"Yes?" She turned back.

Noori was opening something tied to a knot in her dupatta. It was a small paper packet.

Noori handed it to Mona.

"What is—?" Mona was struck silent upon opening the paper packet. It was the silver nose-ring she had bought Noori.

"I'll make up for all your lost jewellery, Mona bibi!" Noori said. "You can deduct the money in instalments from my salary."

"Don't say that!" Mona said, thrusting the nose-ring into Noori's hand. Then she walked away to hide her tears.

MONA LOOKED OUT from the kitchen window when she heard Salamat Ali driving in for lunch.

He saw Noori going to the drawing room with the mop, and came rushing towards her.

"You! Stop there! What are you doing here? Who let you in? Get out of here!"

Noori froze.

Mona came out and signalled to Noori to go inside.

"Salamat, please have a word with me upstairs." She turned and went inside without waiting for his reply.

Salamat Ali stood there for a moment, then thundered in after her and up the stairs.

"What do you mean by this?" he shouted the moment he entered the bedroom. "What is she doing in the house?"

"Keep your voice down, Salamat!" Mona said with great deliberation as she pulled out her dresser chair and sat down to adjust her bun in the mirror. "I've rehired her."

"But it was with good cause we had gotten rid of her!" he snarled. "What am I to understand from this?"

"I don't want to argue. All I'm saying is that I'll be responsible for her actions."

"I don't care. I just don't want her in this house," he said in a firm voice. "Did you hear me, Mona?"

"I heard you." Mona was emboldened by his menacing tone. "She *will* stay!"

He watched her, apparently taken aback by her transformation. She kept fixing her hair.

"So it has come to this, Mona," he said in a hurt tone. "A servant is more important to you than your husband? A liar and a thief!"

Mona looked up at him in the mirror. Her eyes said what her lips did not.

He suddenly fell silent.

She got up and stood watching him for a few moments.

While her instinct convinced her of Noori's innocence, until that moment Mona had had difficulty believing that Salamat Ali was the culprit. She could have forgiven the deed itself. After all, he himself had bought the jewellery for her. What Mona could not forgive was the elaborate deception created by Salamat Ali to incriminate a poor, innocent girl.

Salamat Ali's jaws flexed. He did not return her gaze.

Mona realized now that she had deluded herself by thinking that she had nothing more to lose when she put a stop to the divorce proceedings. She who had always questioned Hina's motives in her actions against Salamat Ali now questioned her own. If Hina had acted out of spite, hadn't she herself acted recklessly? In her defence of Salamat Ali she may have asserted herself before her family, but Salamat Ali himself had seen it as a sign of her vulnerability and begun exploiting it early in their relationship. But she asked herself how wrong she was in doing that. If she took a risk by betting on a relationship with someone like Salamat Ali, her defence of his character was guided by a trust in that relationship.

Mona felt dissatisfied by her reasoning. Wasn't there also a clear desire on her part to act in defiance, she asked herself. The ironic truth did not escape her that in a desire to avenge herself against Akbar Ahmad's injustices, she had been treated as badly or perhaps worse than Akbar Ahmad had treated her. She now believed that what she had been told of Salamat Ali's past was true. But she had too long delayed acting upon that information to use it as a justification now for separation from him. Mona felt her strength failing her. Her confidence was ebbing. She felt she had become the same insecure, unsure Mona she had been all her married life.

She turned away and went into the bathroom, closing the door behind her. She did not want Salamat Ali to see or hear her cry.

Salamat Ali stood staring at the bathroom door, then walked out of the bedroom. He stood on the landing and looked around cautiously as if to make sure there was nobody else in the vicinity. Then he tugged his collar, pulled up his pants, and headed downstairs. Noori, listening at the bottom of the staircase, rushed away before Salamat Ali could see her.

XIII

THE BLACKOUT

Mona did not speak with Sala-mat Ali for three days. Then on the afternoon of the fourth day, he came home for lunch and began talking to her as if nothing had happened. Mona felt a kind of respite. At the moment, she no longer had the energy for—or even an interest in—making efforts to salvage their relationship. She wanted peace.

MONA HAD BEEN PREOCCUPIED and hadn't noticed how bad the weather was. It had rained heavily for a couple of days, the drains had spilled over and the roads were flooded. The generator supplying electricity to the neighbourhood had caught fire and the power supply had broken down for the fourth time in two days. As it was getting dark, Mona lit a few candles. She was in the kitchen making tea for herself when she heard Salamat Ali going out. She had asked him not to go out at night during the storm. He had ignored her.

This was not the first time that she had been alone in the house, but Mona felt restive this evening. After finishing her tea she made some chicken soup and took it to Mrs. Baig, who was ill with a cold. After sitting with her for a while, Mona took her leave and returned home. She telephoned Amber, who gave her news of Kamal's promotion. Amber also told Mona about her latest shopping trip with Tanya. Mona had not heard from Tanya since their confrontation.

When Mona finished talking to Amber, it was close to dinnertime. She ate while watching an old serial that was being rebroadcast on TV.

As Mona was getting ready for bed, the phone rang.

A man's voice said, "Mrs. Salamat Ali?"

"Yes." She thought she heard Salamat Ali in the background, shouting, cursing and breaking into laughter.

"We want you to come and take away your husband."

Mona braced herself. She wondered what had occasioned the call. Salamat Ali had never been in need of being escorted home.

"Can I talk to Salamat Ali?" she asked.

"He can't come to the phone. He is unable to." The caller's manner was evasive.

Mona would have been more frightened had she not heard Salamat Ali's voice. She took down the address before the man hung up.

Mona considered calling Amber to drive her but dismissed the idea as it was too late. She changed her clothes, then took out the umbrella and a raincoat. It was dark and she had to walk in ankle-high water to reach the main road, where she waited nearly half an hour for a taxi.

When Mona arrived at the address given her by the caller, she saw their car parked outside. Salamat Ali sat in it. He honked several times when he saw Mona, then opened the door and struggled to get out. Mona saw a half-empty bottle in his hands.

There were no houses nearby. The taxi driver refused to take Mona back as he was going in another direction. She had to settle with him. A man came out of the house and approached Mona. A few other men watched her from inside the gate.

"Mrs. Salamat Ali?" he asked.

"Yes." She recognized the man's voice. She felt afraid. The street was dark, there was no traffic, and Salamat Ali seemed almost senseless.

"You shouldn't have come, Mona." Salamat Ali said as he came closer to her. "I am perfectly all right. I told them but—"

He stank of alcohol.

"Take him away," the man said. "He has caused enough trouble already."

"I caused trouble . . . ? Let me tell you something—" He waved his finger. "This is no way to treat a member of the club."

"There he goes again," said one of the men standing inside the gate. The others laughed.

"You must understand that a man's word is as good as . . . I just need one more."

The man spoke to Mona in a threatening voice this time. "Take him away immediately." Mona asked him to send someone to fetch a taxi because the main street was several blocks away, but the man went inside and closed the door. The isolated location, the deserted area, the secretive manner of the men—all these factors convinced Mona that it was a gambling den and they did not want Salamat Ali to draw unwanted attention to the place.

"Go and wait in the car, Salamat," she said. "I will go to the main road and find a taxi."

He stood muttering to himself.

As Mona walked towards the main street, she considered her strange dilemma. She was glad she had not brought Amber along. What would Amber have thought of the sordid scene? Salamat Ali was continuously dragging her deeper into his dissipated life. How long would she be able to bear it?

She heard a car behind her.

"Moaaaaaaaana!" Salamat Ali called to her from the driver's seat. "Moaaaaaaaana!" He was now driving alongside her.

"Stop, Salamat! You shouldn't drive now! Stop! Put on the brakes!"

"Get inside!"

"Salamat!!"

"Inside!"

She had no choice; she let him drive. As he mumbled obscenities and threats, she screamed and told him to keep his eyes on the road. Visibility was poor in the darkened streets, and he had difficulty steering around corners.

"They say, 'Unlucky at cards, lucky in love.'" Salamat Ali squeezed her thigh with his hand.

She pushed his hand away.

"What was that place?" she asked after a while. "What happened there tonight?"

He kept making imprecations and did not answer her question. She did not insist. The fresh air seemed to help him to sober slightly. They reached their neighbourhood without mishap.

The streets were still dark. With overcast skies and the fogged windscreen, Salamat Ali could not make out where the road turned. As he lowered the car window to look out, the electric company's repair truck hurtled past, splashing the standing water over him.

Salamat Ali swore loudly. He stopped the car and got out.

Mona tried to pacify him. "Please, Salamat. Quiet down." He continued cursing, but eventually got back into the car and continued driving.

As their car approached their street, Mona saw some overhead electrical wires shorting up ahead. She asked Salamat Ali to slow down. Then she saw the electric company's truck parked near the electrical pole. Technicians stood on the street. One of them was trying to set up the ladder. Salamat Ali saw them too, when the technicians signalled with a flashlight for their car to stop. They were dangerously close to where a jangle of shorting electric wires hung overhead.

Salamat Ali railed at the workers.

"Salamat, what are you doing?" Mona shouted with fear

as the car lurched forward, picking up speed. "Push the brakes! Not the accelerator."

"I'll teach the bastards a nice lesson!"

With horror Mona realized his intention.

One of the technicians tried to get out of the car's path, but he was caught by the side of the car and fell into the standing water. Mona thought he had been killed. She wanted to scream but felt too terrified to utter a sound. Even then, Salamat Ali did not slow down. Mona heard shouts. She saw the figures on the road pass by her vision in a blur. Then she heard Salamat Ali shriek and she turned her head to see the rear of the repair truck looming before them. Mona knew they would die. She felt the impact and heard a deafening sound, and then she lost consciousness.

THE PRICE

Hina and Tanya arrived together at the hospital. Jafar, who had got there first after receiving Mrs. Baig's call, had already phoned the family and reassured them that Mona was not seriously hurt. Amber and her husband arrived last of all because she had to stop on the way to pick up Mrs. Baig. Amber stopped crying only when she saw that her mother was okay.

Mona's X-rays showed no internal injuries. She had a cut on her forehead, which received stitches, and she was told to keep her arm in a sling for a few days. Salamat wore a neck brace for his whiplash injury; he had also dislocated his right shoulder.

At his request, a nurse brought Salamat Ali in a wheelchair to Mona's bedside.

"I want to talk to Mona privately," Salamat Ali said urgently.

Nobody moved. Mona stared straight ahead.

"Mona, ask them to leave."

Mona turned her head away. Amber, who was standing on the other side of her bed, pressed Mona's hand.

"Don't you even want to see how badly I've been hurt, Mona?" Salamat Ali spoke slowly and in a low voice. Mona did not respond. At a glance from Hina, Jafar left the ward.

"She can't talk because she is still in shock from the accident," Salamat Ali said to Amber, who stood before him. "Let us all leave. Let her have some rest. She will talk in the morning."

"I saved your mother, Amber!" Salamat Ali said when he saw that nobody was willing to leave Mona. "I want you to know that. If I had not steered the car away in time and received the full impact myself, she would have broken her neck. Look here! I narrowly escaped death!"

"Don't mention it in front of her now," Amber protested.

"You are right! You are right! But I just don't want you to think that it was my fault."

Just then, Jafar returned with the nurse, who, despite Salamat Ali's protests, wheeled him away.

Mona was released from the hospital the next morning. The doctors were willing to discharge Salamat Ali as well, but he insisted on further medical tests. Because it would take a day for the lab to send the results, he checked himself into a private room for two days.

Upon arriving home Mona was greeted by the portrait of Akbar Ahmad, who wore a smug and vindicated look. As she stood there staring at his face, Habib came in and told her that Salamat Ali had already called, complaining of the hospital food. He was demanding that Mona arrange to send him home-cooked food.

DURING THE NEXT DAY, Mona had her belongings moved into the drawing room. She rearranged the furniture so that there was room for a bed to be placed there for her. The mute anger she had felt at the hospital now turned into a physical revulsion. She was unable to bear even the thought of Salamat Ali's proximity.

On the day Salamat Ali was to be discharged, Mona sent Habib to bring him home in a taxi. She remained in the drawing room while Habib helped Salamat Ali upstairs. Mona could not bring herself to go see Salamat Ali for some time. An hour later, however, she went upstairs to ask him if he needed anything.

"Whatever has been provided for me is more than enough," he said sarcastically. "What more can I possibly need?"

Later in the day, Salamat Ali came down and silently observed Mona's new arrangement. He went upstairs without a comment.

Next day when the physiotherapist made a house call to help him exercise his arm, Mona heard him complaining bitterly of being abandoned by his family in his hour of need, but overall he seemed to accept the estrangement, and after that one incident she did not hear him complain again. He was polite in his dealings with Noori and Habib as well. Mona felt this was because he now depended on them to take care of his meals and his personal needs.

But now Mona felt like a trapped animal. Her move-
ments in her own house had become severely restricted.
As Salamat Ali's presence kept her from going upstairs,
Akbar Ahmad's stare kept her from the living room. She
knew that her makeshift quarters could not be a permanent solution.

One day, as she lay down and was again haunted by
the image of the last few moments before their car hit the
truck, she realized that if she had died then, she would have
done so in a state of profound unhappiness—a condition of
her own creation: she always lost the opportunity to take
her life into her own hands. In Akbar Ahmad's case, at
least, she had had an excuse: she was concerned about the
welfare of her young daughters. But in Salamat Ali's case,
nothing but her own muddled thinking, misguided sense
of self-respect and perhaps a desire to spite Hina and Jafar
had stood in her way.

TWO DAYS AFTER HIS RETURN HOME, Salamat Ali went back to
work. Mona took a taxi to Barrister Huda's office. She had
not informed anyone in advance of her decision. She did not
have the strength to offer explanations.

Barrister Huda did not seem surprised by Mona's
unscheduled visit. If he was, he did not let on. When he
asked Mona why she wanted him to proceed with the case
now, and noticed that Mona had difficulty explaining,
he stopped her.

"I only asked to inquire if there was any material change
in your situation that would have an effect on our filing. I

see that there is none. This is all I need to know. I do not give myself the right to judge your reasoning for the decision."

As she left the office, Mona felt a strange serenity.

She did not want to go home immediately. Instead she spent nearly two hours in the shopping malls on Tariq Road, walking around aimlessly. A salesman in a familiar cosmetics shop invited her in with an offer of a sample of a new cream, and Mona bought it to make him happy. As she was paying, she saw a powder-compact that she had been looking for. She purchased that as well. Later, she stopped by a boutique and purchased herself a cotton sari, and on the way home picked up a pair of matching sandals.

Mona was returning home carrying several shopping bags when she saw Hina's car parked outside her house.

Her sister had been waiting for her in the living room, and came toward her as she saw Mona enter. The moment their eyes met, Mona realized that Hina had found out about the visit to the lawyer. Barrister Huda must have felt a responsibility to inform Jafar.

"Why now, Mona?" Hina began, sounding furious. "How you love to make a spectacle of—" She said no more. Suddenly she looked weary.

Mona, spent, too, sat down without speaking.

They remained silent. After a while, Hina walked over and sat down next to her.

Noori came into the room and looked surprised to see them sitting silently side by side.

"Is everything all right, Mona bibi?" she asked.

Mona smiled faintly.

Noori went away with an anxious look on her face.

"No, you are right," Hina said finally. "The worst that could have happened to you has already happened."

ON THE DAY BARRISTER HUDA was to call at Salamat Ali's office, Mona noticed Salamat Ali dressing with great care. Mona had slept soundly the previous night but now felt anxious. She remained agitated even after the lawyer phoned her around noon and informed her briefly that he was hopeful of executing the divorce. He asked her to come to his office the next morning so that he could give her the details.

Salamat Ali did not return home that night, although someone kept phoning and hanging up well into the early hours of the morning. The last time she picked up the receiver she recognized familiar background noises, the same ones she had heard on the night of the accident when someone had called her to collect Salamat Ali. She disconnected the phone. After that, Mona slept badly.

The next morning in his office, Barrister Huda explained the situation to Mona, who stared at the far wall. "The recent changes in marriage laws have made the divorce process more drawn-out and complicated. It could take well over a year, even without any resistance from either party. The municipal councillors, the civil authorities, all have been given some say in the matter. Mr. Salamat Ali seems well acquainted with the prevailing situation. I also had the impression that he had anticipated some such move on your part."

Mona looked up.

"Yes," continued Barrister Huda, "I think the other party anticipated some such eventuality, because he came well prepared. At any rate, he did not seem at all shocked or surprised. The conditions he stated were well articulated and had been given careful thought. A lawyer could not have made a more cogent presentation. I do not wish to go into the details of his speech at this moment. All you need to know is that he is willing to expedite the process provided an understanding can be reached."

Barrister Huda gave Mona a few papers to study. "Please take your time reading these conditions. I will be back from my lunch break in half an hour."

He got up and began putting on his coat. "We can always negotiate and bargain, but I have a feeling that it will not be—" Barrister Huda stopped, seeing that Mona was already signing the papers. He stood there silently nodding to himself. Then he slowly took off his coat, sat down in his chair, and reached for the stamp pad.

Mona knew that Salamat Ali would never realize how he had unwittingly helped her to repossess herself, and to reclaim her life. The thought troubled her that she would have to live with this lingering feeling of indebtedness towards him. Still, Salamat Ali had eased her conscience about the matter by naming his price. She would be content in the knowledge that he would receive all he thought he deserved from the relationship. As she signed the papers accepting Salamat Ali's conditions, Mona knew that for this feeling of contentment, she would have been willing to part with an even bigger portion of her estate.

~~~

TWO DAYS LATER, Salamat Ali quietly took away his belongings. Mona was at Hina's at the time, and learned about it from Noori upon her return home.

On her own initiative, Noori took down the curtains and washed them along with the bedding. By the next day, with the help of Habib, she had slowly rearranged the whole room.

Even after everything in the bedroom was changed, it was a whole week before Mona could bring herself to go in there.

A DAY LATER, Mona woke up with a high fever. The doctor who visited her could not detect any signs of an infection and attributed her symptoms to fatigue.

Hina stayed by Mona's side while she recuperated. Amber and Tanya spent three days helping to care for their mother. They were relieved by Hina, who took charge of the household once again.

Mona let herself be taken care of. For the first few days, she lay in bed doing nothing. She slept intermittently. A few times, she tried to review all the events of the past several months in her mind, but was unable to do so. Her memory was blank. Mental exhaustion, such as she had never experienced, did not allow her mind to dwell on any subject at length.

After some days, Mona slowly began reconstructing the sequence of events since Akbar Ahmad's death. Sometimes her mind confused the details of Akbar Ahmad's life with her time with Salamat Ali. Sometimes she imagined that Salamat Ali was still in her life, and she relived the anxieties she had recently experienced. She was glad that she had followed through and initiated the divorce proceedings, despite her apprehension as to how others would react to her about-face. She knew what it had taken out of her at a time when she felt emotionally weak and unsure. Her reward was an escape from a nightmare that had, at one point, seemed endless. Mona began to feel a growing sense of freedom, and as the days passed this feeling took root.

There came an afternoon when Mona sat in the garden looking toward the upper storey of Mrs. Baig's house and it did not stir any upsetting thoughts, as if all memories of her recent suffering had been wiped away.

TANYA HAD COME to pick up the containers in which she had brought food while Mona was ill. Mona went into the kitchen to gather them from the cupboard. As she returned to the living room, she saw Tanya staring at the patch on the wall where, until the previous night, Akbar Ahmad's portrait had hung.

Hearing her footsteps, Tanya turned.

After glaring at her mother silently for a moment, Tanya rushed out of the room without taking her dishes and drove away.

The following day, Hina picked Mona up and took her to her house to keep her, in her loneliness, from dwelling on recent events.

Upon her return home a few days later, Mona saw that the patch on the wall had been painted over. She felt glad that the last reminder of Akbar Ahmad's presence had disappeared.

"When did Tanya come by?" Mona asked Noori.

"I didn't see Tanya bibi while you were away," Noori told her. "Only Amber dropped by one day to tidy up the house."

Mona was speechless.

εpiloque

IT WAS NOT in Mrs. Kazi's nature to let a score stand unsettled, especially if it concerned Mona. So when she heard
that Mona was renovating her house, she immediately
announced plans to add an annex to her own house. Then
Mrs. Kazi learned that Imad was supervising the work at
Mona's. Her speculations on the potential scandal of Imad's
presence at Mona's house were disrupted, however, by later
news: Mona was taking driving lessons. The fact of Mona
driving around town while Mrs. Kazi remained a prisoner
to her son's availability was to Mrs. Kazi a catastrophe, and
posed such a direct and palpable threat that Mrs. Kazi, too,
enrolled in a neighbourhood driving school. To spite
Mona, she insisted that Tanya take her on practice drives.

Mona noticed when Akbar Ahmad's portrait resurfaced
in Tanya's house, but it did not reawaken agonizing memories. Akbar Ahmad was there only in a father's role and
presented himself as such to Mona.

Mona's relationship with Tanya remained difficult. But just as she was too busy with her life to heed Mrs. Kazi's machinations, she had also become somewhat less involved in her daughters' lives, and less dependent on their presence.

Mona accompanied Mrs. Baig to the women's club meetings and drove her to offices on her social work errands, though they continued their weekday walks. When they tired of the neighbourhood park, for a change of scene they drove to other recreational areas or to the beach.

Once when she was walking by the shore with Mrs. Baig, Mona had a distinct feeling that she was being watched. It was a strangely familiar feeling. It reminded her of Salamat Ali watching her from his balcony with his binoculars. Involuntarily she turned to look. It was a weekend and the beach was crowded with people who had come out to escape the oppressive heat. Mona could not determine who, if anyone, was observing her. She had not received any news of Salamat Ali. He seemed to have disappeared.

One evening, several days after the house renovations were finished, Imad came over for tea. He returned the next week and the next, and soon his weekly visits became routine. In the beginning, Mona wondered how the course of her life might have changed if Hina had persuaded her to marry him instead. She felt no regrets now; she had become accustomed to making decisions to suit her own priorities. Even the best of marital relationships, she knew, did not offer that liberty. Independence was something that she wished to maintain; moments of loneliness were a small price to pay.

Mona looked forward to Imad's visits. She knew she enjoyed them more because they always came to an end.

Author's Note

THE PORTRAIT THAT INSPIRED this story hangs in a house in Toronto. My wife, Michelle, and I saw it when visiting an octogenarian gentleman and his third wife, whose first husband had been dead for many years; his portrait hung directly above her current husband's rocking chair. She told us that when getting married she had made it clear that the portrait would stay and that her husband-to-be had happily consented. While he was telling us of his many adventures with women, the portrait surveyed the room with a magisterial air, and I wondered what kind of relationship existed between the two gentlemen: one in the chair and the other in the frame. My thoughts soon became the story of the widow and her new husband. I told it to my friend and editor Bob Wyatt who read it in several drafts and advised me, giving it a sharper focus, which greatly improved this story. As always, I am grateful to my agents, Elaine and Tom Colchie, for their enthusiasm and support.

Michael Schellenberg, my editor at Knopf Canada, went over the story, knocked it about, and offered many wonderful suggestions. Among them was his discovery that Salamat Ali could be made even naughtier.

My copy editor, Allyson Latta, purged its remaining sins.

Finally, I am indebted to the superb team at Random House of Canada Limited: Louise Dennys, Diane Martin, and Marion Garner, whose warm-hearted support for this story made the book possible.

MUSHARRAF ALI FAROOQI is an author and translator. His critically acclaimed translation of the Indo-Islamic epic *The Adventures of Amir Hamza* was published by the Modern Library in 2007. He has also translated the works of contemporary Urdu poet Afzal Ahmed Syed. He is also the author of a children's picture book, *The Cobbler's Holiday or Why Ants Don't Wear Shoes*. Musharraf Ali Farooqi was born in 1968 in Hyderabad, Pakistan, and lives in Toronto.

Visit the author's website, www.MAFarooqi.com, for more information about his other works.